What the critics are saying

"This thrilling story is filled with passion, danger, customs and hope. I excitedly look forward to reading the rest of Windsor's Arda collection." - *Romantic Times, four stars*

"...One of the best examples of the blending of romance and erotica this reviewer has seen...a MUST read for romantica fans!" - *The Romance Studio, four and one-half hearts*

"...an intergalactic medley of good and evil, passion and peril, and the best magic of all...love! ...a read I'd recommend!" - *A Romance Review, four roses*

"...Simply stunning. Annie Windsor's writing is fresh and witty, easily capable of capturing the reader's attention. But be careful with this book, as you'll lose all track of time..." - *Escape to Romance, four and one-half roses*

"*The Sailmaster's Woman* is one hot read! Halfway through this erotic love story, I was praying to be kidnapped, then saved by sexy aliens with voracious appetites for women. Ms. Windsor has created a world where pleasure knows no bounds, and inhibitions are left at the door...not to be missed!" - *Romance Reviews Today*

"A scorcher of the highest magnitude...magnificent world...amazing characters...I highly recommend *Arda: The Sailmaster's Woman*, and not just because of the unforgettably tantalizing love scenes...This is one novel I'll be rereading very soon, while I impatiently await the sequel..." - *In the Library Reviews*

"Unique, wonderful, spellbinding, crazy, erotic...This is a science fiction work, but just as easily one of fantasy and I would recommend it for the lovers of both. Personally, I think anyone with a taste for true love, only love, would enjoy this...Expect a hot read in this one folks because they don't come with much more fire!" —*Timeless Tales, five stars*

"Annie Windsor takes the reader on a wild ride through space and time. Her loves scenes are incredibly erotic, her characters both strong and resilient, and her descriptions of the far off reaches of space enchanting. This book definitely earns five ice cubes for erotic content, so enjoy." - *Romance Junkies, five ice cubes*

"A very sexy adventure...whiz-bang start to the series. Ki is a delicious hero, and his single-minded pursuit of his soul's mate is enough to make any woman wish to be in Elise's place... THE SAILMASTER'S WOMAN is a sexy adventure that any fan of romantica will enjoy, but one that will capture the heart of those who enjoy futuristic romance." – *Sensual Romance Reviews*

"Powerful, pulsating and perfect is this masterfully written tale by Annie Windsor. The characters in this tale are witty, explosive, loyal and sinfully sensual! Elise and Ki are a strong, loving couple who burn up the pages and readers won't be able to get enough of them... Annie Windsor is a shining star in erotic romance who will captivate you, make you dream and wish to be THE SAILMASTER'S WOMAN!" - *Road to Romance*

ELLORA'S CAVE
ROMANTICA PUBLISHING

Arda: The Sailmaster's Woman
An Ellora's Cave publication, 2003

Ellora's Cave Publishing, Inc.
PO Box 787
Hudson, OH 44236-0787

ISBN # 1843607379

ISBN MS Reader (LIT) ISBN # 1-84360-385-3
Other available formats (no ISBNs are assigned):
Adobe (PDF), Rocketbook (RB), Mobipocket (PRC) & HTML

Edited by Ann Richardson.
Cover art by Christine Clavel.

ARDA:
THE SAILMASTER'S WOMAN

Annie Windsor

Chapter 1

Elise Ashton rubbed her blue eyes and yawned as her cousin Georgia Steel sat down across from her.

The sidewalk café was packed. A dozen yellow plastic tables, two dozen yellow chairs, a brick patio, and a hundred coffee-seeking zombies—it was almost too much for Elise's senses after a sleepless weekend.

She gazed first at Georgia's tired face and then at the sky, wishing she could soar into the low-hanging clouds and escape to Polaris, or maybe Cassiopeia. If only space travel were possible. Surely those star systems had life-sustaining planets, and surely their inhabitants were more interesting than Nashville's natural species: Genus Redneckius.

Then again, if Elise's First Rule held true, the Milky Way wouldn't offer her much better fare than Middle Tennessee.

Elise's First Rule: In the end, all men are boring.

In front of her, gray city streets bustled with typical Monday traffic. Morning heat rose from the pavement in shimmering waves, punctuated by car exhaust and hurrying pedestrians.

"This place looks more like New York every day," Elise muttered. Her long blond hair already lay limp against her shoulders, a testament to July's blistering temperatures.

"Amen." Georgia brushed red bangs behind her ears. The heat didn't seem to be affecting her, but it never did.

Georgia was one of those perfect women with a tiny waist, sparkling green eyes, and slender hips. One of those women who worried over losing half a pound, and how many calories were in a carrot stick. If Elise hadn't loved her distant cousin like a sister, she probably would have spiked Georgia's coffee with the highest calorie chocolate syrup *Coffee Stand* had to offer.

A waitress in a white t-shirt with "Latté" scrawled across her plastic-enhanced chest minced over, flashed a phony smile, plopped two cups on their table, and left without so much as a boo or how-do-you-do.

Elise glared after Latté-tits and sighed. "This freaky-dream thing is out of hand. If I don't get some sleep, I'm likely to pour espresso on that woman's head. Perky and rude should be an illegal combination."

"Mm. Well, I think your sexual repression is getting to you." Georgia downed a swig of her morning rations.

"I'm not repressed." Elise shifted in her plastic chair, bringing her knees together and smoothing her black business skirt. It was an unconscious gesture, and Georgia caught it before Elise did.

"Scared something's gonna crawl up in there, girl?"

"No!" Elise let her legs fall open for three seconds, then snapped them back together again. "I mean, not anything I don't want."

Georgia leaned forward, exposing shameless cleavage. "And what does Elise Ashton really, really, gotta-have-it-'til-her-clit-aches want?"

For a few seconds, Elise couldn't speak. Her neck felt warm enough to combust, and she squeezed her coffee mug until her fingers burned. "Oh, please. Let's not start this so early. I'm too sleepy to defend myself."

"You're such a wimp."

"Am not."

"When was the last time you did something wild?"

"I—you—oh, fuck you. Drink your coffee."

Georgia settled back in her seat, bouncing her foot like she usually did after whipping Elise in an argument.

If she hadn't been so sluggish, Elise would have given that bouncing foot a good flick, or at least kicked at one of Georgia's plastic chair legs. Her recent Tai Kwon Do lessons might have made that interesting. As it was, she just smiled at her cousin, filed the exchange for later revenge, and went back to yawning.

"I think it's a trust thing." Georgia grinned. Her foot was still bouncing. "You've been screwed over so many times, you figure why bother, right?"

"Elise's Second Rule: Trust no one but Georgia." Elise sipped at her mocha-almond express, wishing it were magical elixir. "Besides, you've had your own share of screw-overs, m'dear. Face it. Good men, the kind of men who can handle a strong-minded woman—don't exist."

Georgia sighed. "Pessimist. You're probably right, but I'm not willing to give up yet."

Elise took another slug of her espresso, hoping it would keep her eyes open. The State of Tennessee would be grateful if she stayed awake to log in the endless complaints received by the Attorney General's office. No doubt Georgia would be grateful, too, as Elise would be quicker to grab one of the ringing phones. Bossing high-level politicians and lawyers all day kept Elise's mental and emotional claws sharpened, and she could use the workout today.

Georgia and Elise had manned the AG's secretarial staff for almost ten years, since they both finished high school and opted out of college. Georgia didn't go on to higher education because she hated school. Elise didn't go because she couldn't afford it. She meant to try again once she got older, to study her true passion of astronomy, but there was work. And bills. And Georgia's endless tales of woe from failed relationships. Georgia needed Elise, and Elise needed to be there for her cousin.

Elise's Third Rule: Always take care of Georgia, because she's all you've got.

The two women had grown up together with their only surviving aunt, with little knowledge of their family. As far as Elise was concerned, they hadn't done badly for themselves, either.

At twenty-eight, Elise didn't know if she could even handle the studying involved with going back to school—the grading, the long hours, or even the change from her comfortable, quiet life. She still had her constellation charts and the telescope she bought when she was only twelve. She didn't use it much any more, but every now and then, in the tiny hours of night, when she was almost sure no one could see her, she'd steal a glance at a comet, or watch a meteor shower.

And as the magnificent events unfolded, she would give in to her natural excitement, using her vibrator to bring herself to quick, sharp orgasms as the heavens sparkled.

Now that was something wild.

At least it broke the monotony. But she would never admit it to anyone—especially Georgia. The two women shared an odd instinct, a connection that often let them know more about each other than they should. Elise figured the closeness came from growing up virtually alone, but Georgia always said they were secretly the children of psychic gods.

Whatever.

Elise wasn't spilling about her vibrator or her personal falling stars.

"So, is it still the same dream?" Georgia's lyrical voice cut beneath the crowd noise.

"Yes. Well, no." Elise shifted in her chair, not wanting to lie, but not wanting to mention the nightmares that had recently intruded on her fantasy dreams. In the nightmares, she was a slave, riding in a squalid ship made to look like an inhuman skull. Elise's dreams had a habit of coming true, though not always directly. They were like hints of the future, and the skull-slave scene was definitely not one she wanted to talk about.

"Tell." Georgia leaned forward. Her bright green eyes almost glittered. "I know those dreams are hot."

Elise forced a smile. "Not hot, really. But definitely more intense."

She let the warm coffee run down her throat between sentences. The sensation was almost wicked, especially when paired with thoughts about her nighttime stargazing, and her *good* dreams. The ones about the space pirate with midnight hair and obsidian eyes. Orion himself, with muscles like a god, standing astride the deck of his silver space frigate. Him, she could fuck all night.

"I keep waking up at the wrong times, though." Elise sighed. "Just before the handsome guy makes me come."

"I think you should see your doctor." Georgia glanced at her watch. "Come on. We'll be late."

Elise stood, thinking that if she told her doctor anything about her dreams and fantasies, he'd either take her right there on the exam table or send her to a shrink.

The doc was cute, but he didn't warm Elise's engines. Given that he was rich, smart beyond reason, and very handsome, her lack of response suggested the shrink might be a good idea.

In the end, all men are boring.

However, the thought of being examined with an intimate twist not only made Elise's heart beat faster, but it brought a quick, throbbing ache to the celestial equator between her legs. It had been too long since someone explored her galaxy.

And it was damned hard to find an explorer who knew how to navigate.

If she could find a man, one true, honest man who could excite her every night—a man who would respect her, yet stand up to her—she would wrap her legs tight around that man, fuck him blind, and never let go.

For a few blocks, Elise and Georgia walked in silence as Elise pondered the fact that her standards were so high most men no longer interested her. *In the end…boring.*

Even the good ones. Not that the few relationships she suffered through could be counted as "good ones," but still.

What was she waiting for?

Did she think Orion would drop out of the sky and sweep her away for hot sex on his star boat?

Yeah, right.

Stupid. Exciting, but stupid.

Even if space pirates existed, Elise doubted that any of them would seek wanton sex with her. She just wasn't the type men picked for a wild fucking, no matter how racy her private fantasies became. She was a woman who hooked up with "nice" guys. Clunky, quiet, reserved businessmen who had no clue what to do with a car engine or a clit. Like Bob at work, her supervisor. He'd been making eyes at her for years, and he'd made it clear that if Elise got ready for launch, he was standing by.

Bob was handsome in that former-linebacker sort of way, but jeez. He defined boring, like most men did, in the end, as her first rule so clearly summarized.

Now, Orion—he might be another story.

Enough. Elise forcefully ignored the ache between her legs. *I can't spend my whole day lost in sexual daydreams.*

As her attention returned to reality, she could feel the rush hour crowd jostling by. The air was only getting hotter in the forest of downtown high-rises, and the whole scene made Elise long for a quick trip to the moon.

Instead, she turned left with Georgia, into the alley between two of the tallest government buildings in Nashville. As Georgia cleared the crowd, a man bumped her arm and spilled her coffee all over her blouse.

He didn't even slow down.

Georgia stood stock still for a second, staring after him in disbelief.

Elise noticed the curve of her cousin's perfect breast, nipple hardening beneath the hot liquid. The rich smell of coffee filled her senses, and she wondered what Georgia looked like when she climaxed. Both of her nipples were probably huge then, swollen after so much kneading and sucking.

How would it feel to be fucked by one of the gorgeous male specimens who were never too far from Georgia's beck and call?

Georgia was so free. So reckless.

She probably wore those men out.

Georgia caught Elise's eye, and for one dignity-shattering moment, Elise believed her cousin was reading her mind. She felt her cheeks blaze, hotter than the images still flickering on her mental screen.

A sly grin played on Georgia's elfin features. "Penny for your thoughts."

Elise wished desperately that her face would quit burning. "Not for a million bucks."

What's the matter with me?

"Girl, sometimes, I have the distinct feeling you're wilder than you let on." Georgia grinned again, then sighed and pulled the wet fabric away from her still-saluting nipple. "It's gonna be a hell-Monday. I can tell."

The flames ebbed out of Elise's face. She reached for her bag to get a napkin to help Georgia dry off, then realized there was nothing hanging from her shoulder. "Damn! I must have left my purse at the café. At the counter, when I paid." She stomped her foot. "Damn, damn, damn!"

Georgia looked at her watch. "We don't have time to go back. Five minutes—we'll lose points."

"You head on inside." Elise pointed to the entrance. "I'll run back for it. I can afford a few points to save my license and credit cards."

"Okay, but—hey, I know." Georgia's mischievous smile was unmistakable. "I'll tell Bob you were having female problems. That'll shut him up. He'll probably forget to dock you for being late."

Once more, heat rose to Elise's cheeks at the image of good old Bob thinking about her private bodily functions. "Gee. Thanks. What a true friend."

Georgia giggled, then hurried into the building.

Elise turned and jogged toward the alley entrance. Rush hour was waning. She should be able to get to the café and back in just a few minutes. Bob would have to deal with it. No way was she leaving her wallet—

Smash!

Elise had struck something rock-solid.

She fell hard on her backside, scraping her hands on the dirty alley stones. Pain coursed her spine, and her palms burned.

Legs.

There were legs in front of her, eight to be exact, blocking the alley entrance.

And they looked like leather-clad tree trunks.

The air popped, as if a bubble had dropped around Elise, blocking out the typical city noises and sights. She couldn't see people or cars. There was nothing outside the alley. And nothing in it but her and the tree-trunk legs.

Harsh laughter filled the air.

Elise's heart thundered as she raised her eyes.

Oh, God.

These weren't pirates. At least not the dreamy kind.

The tree-legged men were enormous. Easily seven feet tall, dressed in slick bodysuits and armed with weird silver sticks topped by glowing crescents. And they weren't handsome guys. To a one, they looked like carnival freak shows, human but scale-covered. Long fingernails, spiked teeth—maybe they were part lizard. Or part alligator.

Who could tell?

One thing was for sure, though.

They had skulls tattooed on their scaly necks, and they were green. As in Crayola green.

What are these guys? Actors? Movie monsters?

Elise scrambled to her feet, unable to keep from staring.

The monster closest to her pulsed like a heartbeat, from plain green to neon green and back again. If that was a special effect, it was more advanced than any film crew in Nashville could afford.

But if they aren't actors…

Elise's mouth went dry. The neon alligator's stick was huge. Bigger than all the rest, with a double-crescent tip. He was twice as ugly as his companions, with scratches and gashes and bald patches on his scaled skin.

An alligator with mange. And some freaky cattle prod.

Elise tried to back away, and ran into leather and metal.

She didn't turn around. Somehow, seeing more alligators behind her would have taken her sanity.

Her chest was so tight she couldn't breathe or speak, but in the next second, she heard herself whisper, "What—I mean—who are you?"

More alligator laughter polluted the alley. It sounded like saws on concrete, and Elise became aware of a swampy, stale smell. It was…dirty. The kind of odor she imagined to fill the back rooms of porno shops and peep shows.

Before Elise could regain her mental balance, the pulsing neon alligator reached a claw forward and flicked the end of her nipple.

"Ow!" Fury surged through her, and she dropped into a Tai Kwan Do ready pose. "Bastard! Wanna try that again?"

The monster lunged, and Elise kicked.

He dodged her blow easily and grinned, bringing the tip of his stick around to tap her behind.

Elise screamed as a burning pulse shot through her muscles.

"What the hell is that thing?" She pivoted to the side of the stick and landed a punch on the bastard's nose. For nothing. He didn't even flinch.

One of the creeps shocked her from behind, and the pain was excruciating.

Tears leaped into her eyes, and she swore under her breath. No way was she crying in front of these freaks. Clawed fingers closed on her shoulders. Again, she tried to defend herself, but her captor was too strong. And those shock sticks—they were inches away. She didn't dare move too much.

One of the alligators snapped a cold metal collar around her neck.

"Damn you!" She grabbed the band with both hands and pulled at it, but it shocked her just like the sticks did.

More scaly hands clamped on her arms and jerked her backward. Scaly arms wrapped around her, crushing air from her lungs.

Elise worked to kick but couldn't get off a good blow. Her heart was in open rebellion, hammering against her ribs. She screamed, but her throat closed off the sound.

"No one can hear you," said the alligator with mange. He was lurking in front of her, double-crescent stick inches from her right cheek, and a hungry, taunting expression twisting his greenish lips.

Elise had the distinct sensation that her collar had just told her what the monster said. Even the horror of her situation couldn't block the wonder of that fact.

Reality began to sink in.

These—these—*things* were aliens, and she was suddenly closer to the stars than she had ever been. The skulls on their necks—her nightmare!

Whatever was happening to her, it wasn't going to be pleasant.

A sharp pain lanced her forearm. A shot. They had given her some sort of shot.

She tried to pull away, but claws dug farther into her shoulder.

Colors rose and swam at the edges of her vision, and she felt her muscles deny her terror and begin to relax.

"Who are you?" she asked again, slurring her words.

The mangy alligator leaned close to her, nearly gagging her with his sex-shop reek. With two rough fingers, he grabbed Elise's chin and kept her from turning away as he spoke in a voice more gravel than sound.

"My name is Gith. Lord Gith. But you will call me Sir. We are your new masters, wench."

He gave her arm a tweak with his stick, and the pain was searing. Mind-boggling. Amplified by the collar around her neck.

Elise's eyelids fluttered once, then closed.

* * * * *

Ki Tul'Mar swung his sword in a wide arc, feeling night's shroud fall away from his mind.

The *Kon'pa,* a spiritual dance to honor the stars, the sails, and *pa*—the living essence that connected all things—was an ingrained part of his morning routine. Each step fell carefully on the silvery *pa*-coated floor of his quarters, and each movement served the balance of his diamond blade. A perfect weapon, carved from the jewels on Andromeda, and set in a hilt of the finest steel his home planet Arda had to offer.

Arda was famous for metallurgy, fine castles, magnificent Chimera beasts, and towering warriors. In all of the galaxy, no planet had such a fine and honorable reputation, and no planet had such an ample supply of *pa*. Upholding Arda's standards was Ki's mission and purpose. He was the Sailmaster, a more absolute ruler than any king, and the title both pleased and burdened him.

Ki's muscles stretched, working out stiffness and damage from the last week of battles. The OrTans had grown bold indeed, raiding and sacking planets in the primitive sectors to fill their skull ships with new pleasure-slaves. Intergalactic laws the Ardani warriors had sworn to uphold, to defend and enforce to the last ship, sword, and man in the Royal Fleet, forbade this.

Ki bared his teeth and growled, once more whipping his diamond blade through the cabin's lavender half-light. Around him, in a circle on the warm stone floor, candles flickered. His steps never overturned a single flame, despite his incredibly long and powerful stride. On his chest, his *pa*-mark tingled, traveling in its flame pattern toward his shoulders.

Now in his full physical prime, Ki could walk a railing on his toes, sword battle in a crow's nest, or take on ten OrTans with only his blade for a companion. He could run a castle battlement faster than any of his crew, storm a fortress on the back of Artur, his graceful Chimera, and keep the unquestioning loyalty and support of millions in the Arda system—and beyond. Even throughout the Galactic Council worlds.

He had awards and gifts of honor. He had fans and admirers and followers. He had a strong, vibrant *pa*-mark, and *Astoria,* the finest frigate in the Fleet.

Yes. Ki Tul'Mar had everything an honorable Sailmaster could desire.

Except a soul's mate.

With a forceful lunge, he thrust his diamond blade forward to finish *Kon'pa*. Sweat covered him like a damp robe, and his breath came in even, determined drafts. His teeth were still clenched, and the thought of his failure to find a mate rankled in his gut even as he counted his many blessings.

But why should he care? He had service for his warrior's needs any time he chose to avail himself of the flocks of ready females. And he could seek his soul's mate any time he set his mind to the task. It was a terrible risk, but the Law of Keeping caused him little fear. He had no doubt he could win the woman, if ever he chose to locate her.

For now, he did not choose to look. He did not need a *shanna*. Why would any warrior want to be distracted from Fleet duties, desire to be besotted and frenzied like some adolescent fool?

Even if I searched, I could find no woman worth that kind of energy.

Before Ki could continue with his private concerns, Fari's psi voice intruded.

Mind your thoughts, you oversized blowhard.

Ki's eyes narrowed. Even Sailmasters were cursed with younger brothers. Arrogant whelps who bedded every twist and wiggle from Celestia to the Galactic Council's back chambers. No doubt Fari, the Sailkeeper of Arda, would have chosen a mate ten stellar years ago, fulfilled the Law, and pumped her with enough seed to breed a dozen heirs.

"Mind your own thoughts," Ki grumbled to Fari, thinking it much louder than he said it. "And ram your overactive staff into a board while you do."

To his great annoyance, laughter answered him. *I had favor enough from our latest rescues to spare me the splinters. You, on the other hand, when was your last coupling, brother?*

Ki didn't answer. He didn't have to. Fari knew well that his older brother had his pick of the willing rescues, who had serviced the Sailmaster well and quickly.

Battle-weary from stellar days of combat with the OrTan, Ki had welcomed the touch of women and the relief of climax. All four women had been beautiful. Various species of females, mostly humanoid—but none captured his interest for longer than their hands or mouths worked his mast, or for longer than they could accommodate his warrior's length in their warm, wet sanctuaries. He had given them all as much pleasure as they could tolerate, and sent them on their way.

Then, as he had so many nights, he had dreamed of a woman, as fine and beautiful as those described in Arda's ancient legend of the *Lorelei*. The mythical guardians of the Tul'Mar line. Now those were women of great intelligence and fierceness, and power beyond reckoning, if legends could be believed.

The *Lorelei* were halflings, part primitive human and part Ardani, wild with psi-power and rumored to be skilled in sorcery. The legends warned of *Lorelei* slipping through the forests about the Tul'Mar castle, prowling for traitors and saboteurs.

Perhaps every warrior secretly wished to bed a *Lorelei* and discover that such an astonishing female was his soul's mate.

To Ki's knowledge, this had never happened.

Perhaps the woman of whom he dreamed was his fantasy mate, a *shanna* who would give herself to him without sucking away his sanity and focus. In his sleep, he had touched her fine curves and flaxen curls, and he had kissed her eyes—as blue and bright as Andromeda's finest gems. As blue as the blade he carried at his side.

Perhaps your diamond-eyed Lorelei *is hidden among the fergilla back on Arda,* Fari mused, interrupting Ki's train of thought. *Those beasts have little psi ability, so I could well understand how you might miss her in the herd—*

Only you would know if fergilla have genitals. No doubt you've bedded your share of their hairy arses, too.

Fari was quiet for a moment, not making use of the psi connection so closely shared by those of the same blood, or by soul's mates.

Ki sheathed his sword and waved a hand over the ring of candles. The flames snuffed, filling the cabin with the scent of spices and wood. He breathed deeply, letting the calming vapors wash through him before he went to find Fari, at which point he intended to toss him overboard.

You might ask the heavens for strength enough to pitch me into the void, but it would be only that, brother. Fari's thoughts were gentle, but mocking. *Prayers.*

"You will be needing prayers when I find you." Ki flexed an arm, closed his fist, and imagined his little brother's throat in his neat grasp. His *pa* surged. He could use a good sparring.

Ki. Fari's mental tone changed from teasing to hard in an instant. From brother to Sailkeeper with barely a breath. *Activity in Sector B. Three skulls, heading away from the third planet.*

A quick storm of rage blew through Ki. *How did they get through perimeter patrols?*

I do not know, brother.

"By the worlds." Ki's hand dropped to the hilt of his diamond blade even as his mind reached out to the celestial mainsail's vibrant *pa* fabric. "About. Come about!"

Chapter 2

Elise woke slowly, a black veil of stupor lifting off her brain.

For a moment, she thought she was in her own bed, but the feel of silk against her naked skin told another story. Raising her hands, she touched her breasts.

There was no silk between her palms and her nipples.

Feeling around, she realized there was nothing at all but her, and she was floating. Rolling first to the left, then to the right, Elise determined she was lying on soft, drifting air. Wherever she was, it was pitch dark, and it smelled like roses and sandalwood. She decided the too-strong scent was incense or smoke, carried to her in brief, strong spurts—like an air freshener. A low thrumming sound rumbled in the background, and every few seconds, the room vibrated.

Like an airplane.

"Oh, God." Elise sat up, grabbing the metal collar around her neck. She gave it a small tug, and a warning prod of pain traveled her spine.

"I'm on a spaceship. I'm a prisoner." She let go of the collar. "No. That's ridiculous. I've got to be dreaming."

But her unusually sharp instincts were supercharged, and somehow, she *knew* she wasn't in a movie, or dreaming, or imagining. This was real. She was on a spaceship. For half a second, she was thrilled, and then terrified.

Those alligators—Their pain sticks…

"Hello? Is anyone here?"

Her voice sounded small against the background hum.

Where were her ugly kidnappers?

No one answered her, and suddenly, Elise was cold. No sooner did she think about the chill than the air supporting her warmed until she was comfortable. Except for the fact that she was naked, and the air was brushing her breasts with tongue-like gusts.

Oh, no. Not possible. She couldn't get aroused after being kidnapped by alligator freaks.

Elise covered herself, and the air tickled the backs of her hands. In her palms, her nipples felt like marbles. And the air was starting on her toes, her feet, her calves, and up, to her thighs. A perfect pressure, like fingers made of feathers. Her face heated up, and she had to keep reminding herself that she was alone in total darkness.

At least she hoped she was alone, especially as the air slipped between her legs and began a lazy massage, pushing through her lips to her shielded slit and teasing her clit until she moaned.

For a few seconds, Elise tried to fight the exotic softness, but it was no use. Her body began to drift in a slow spin, responding to her every gasp and shudder as the air moved up and back, then around in circles, pushing and releasing her wet, swollen clit until she cried out again. Every nerve in her body was humming with the motion of the ship, with the relentless air, now wickedly parting her legs.

An image of Orion popped into Elise's mind, and the air became the pirate's hands. His tongue. His hot, welcome weight pressing against her. His fingers taunting her pussy until she groaned and threw open her legs. Sandalwood and roses filled her senses, no longer too strong, now blending with the strokes of the thick, solid air as it thrust into her.

The first orgasm took her by storm, washing every inch of her in delicious shivers. `And the air just kept fucking her. She came a second time, just as intense and leaving her rattled and whimpering, wishing she had her Orion in her arms.

At that, the air became wonderfully solid. She had something to hold, and damned if it didn't feel just like she thought Orion would. Hard and unyielding, yet gentle, and so incredibly warm.

The air slipped behind her, as if cradling her in a loving embrace.

Light seared through the room.

Elise tried to cover herself, but the air was holding her too tightly. Her breath came in sharp gasps as her eyes adjusted—to a window opening before her.

It showed an empty room.

Hot with embarrassment, with the flush of her climaxes, and from the firm feel of the air once more teasing her nipples, Elise gaped as a woman entered the room—no! Not a woman.

Well, not a human woman.

She was naked except for a silver collar, with flaming red hair like Georgia, and perky breasts. Four of them. The hair between her legs was bushy auburn, and when she turned toward Elise, she reclined back in mid-air, running her six-fingered hand between her legs.

Elise bit her lip, wishing she could vanish, but the woman didn't seem to see her.

A man entered next, very handsome and sculpted—normal looking except for his height, his faint green color, and the incredible length of his prick.

Dear God. It must be fourteen inches. And he isn't even hard yet!

Fascinated and horrified, Elise stared as the man stepped behind the woman and began fondling her breasts. His unusual color and muscled arms stood out against her smooth white flesh and the swelling red of her nipples. The woman closed her eyes. Her lips parted, and Elise imagined that she was sighing or moaning. Elise was sighing and moaning, too, as the air was mimicking the green man's gentle pinches.

Elise twisted in her silken prison, but the air held her fast, kissing her skin as the man dragged his lips over the woman in the room. As his tongue circled her nipples, the air licked at Elise's rock-hard buds. She moaned in spite of herself and forgot her guilt as the man moved to the side, took one of the woman's breasts in his mouth, and began to suck. Softly at first, then harder, nipping and tugging.

The sensation went on and on, with Elise knowing she was feeling everything the woman felt. The blend of fear and wonder and complete anonymity turned something loose inside Elise, and she thrust her breasts higher, just as the woman was doing. She groaned, no doubt mimicking the woman's cries of pleasure.

By the time the man plunged his long fingers into the woman's pussy, Elise's mind was spinning. She was more aroused than she had ever been, thrashing and nearly begging the air to finish.

"Please," she gasped as the woman grabbed the man's enormous prick and guided it toward her center. "Please!"

He penetrated the woman fast and hard, just as the air penetrated Elise. Pain shot through her and she screamed—and the air eased back out just as the man was easing out of the screaming woman.

He's so big. Relax. Damn. I've got to relax.

With a slow release of breath, she willed her body to cooperate.

When the man entered the woman's pussy again, it was a gentle stroke, and Elise found that she could take the length and size of the air pushing inside her. She moved until she could receive it comfortably, and the air and the man began a slow, rhythmic pumping.

Each thrust brought Elise to the very edge of pleasure and pain. She closed her eyes, rolling her hips high to meet what had once more become her vision of Orion.

"I want you," she moaned. "Harder. More. I need you!"

The air hammered away, rubbing through her juices, driving her near to madness until her climax exploded like a flare. "I need you! Yes. Yes!"

In that instant of bliss, Elise felt a tickling in her mind. Like a touch, only sharper and deeper. A probe. It hurt for a moment, and then she was lost to the waves of sensation, watching the green man and the red-headed woman grind, heads thrown back with the force of their delight.

The window went dark, and Elise startled at her sudden isolation.

The air that had pleased her so thoroughly now lowered her gently to the ship's cool floor, and slipped into nothingness.

Elise's legs wobbled. She thought about sitting down, but the ship slowed, pitching her backward into a cold metal wall. She landed on her bare backside so hard her teeth clicked together.

The thrumming sound grew louder, and she thought she could hear shouting and clanking. Dull thumps echoed from somewhere. The sandalwood and rose air-freshener was replaced by puffs of what smelled like burning rubber and flaming hair.

Elise's chest tightened.

She covered herself with her hands, then wondered what the hell she was doing. What did it matter if anyone saw her? She trusted nothing in the world except Georgia—save for her own instincts. And her instincts told her something was wrong. More than wrong.

The room was heating up like an oven. She had to get out of there.

Her feet slipped and slid as she stood, but she managed to get both hands pressed against the now-warm walls. Walking slowly, she ran her fingers up and down the smooth metal, looking for a weak spot she could use her martial arts training to kick or punch open.

There was nothing. Not even a seam or a bolt.

As she felt around where she was sure the window had been, a sudden bang and flare of brightness made her whirl around, hands raised and ready to fight.

Her eyes ached, then teared as light and smoke stung them. This was no observation window. Someone had opened a door.

A huge, ugly figure thundered toward her through the haze. It was one of her kidnappers. Gith. The alligator with mange, holding his double-crescent stick.

"Wench!" he bellowed, stopping inches from her as she cowered back, hands still raised. "I choose you for my own prize, begin your breaking-in gently—no pain stick flailings, no time with the troops—I gave you my own *gasha* bed, even. And this is the thanks I receive?"

He raised his claws, swirling smoke around them.

"W-What?" Elise glanced under both of his arms, judging her odds of escape. If she could hit him once, right in the nose—

"Do not play with me!" The alligator snatched her off the ground by her neck, bringing his stick within inches of her cheek. She smacked his arms, but she might as well have been punching stone. "I know you called to your Ardani lover with your mind. We picked it up on our psi scanners, just before the Fleet attacked."

Elise kept pounding the alligator's scaly arm. She had no idea what he was talking about, but he was cutting off her air. Pain twisted through her neck, and her stomach ached with the effort of breathing.

"Call him off." The alligator increased the pressure on her throat and gave her the first taste of his horrible shock stick. "Tell him to leave my ship, or I will snap you in half and cook your guts for a feast!"

* * * * *

Ki fought like a man possessed. His *pa*-mark sizzled beneath his loose tunic, burning him and spurring him onward. OrTans fell like foul rain at his feet. Pain sticks flew and broke like toothpicks. His diamond blade slashed again and again, wasting beast and rigging and portal—anything in his way as he fought toward the center of the skull ship.

Down, past the troops and guards. Down, through the bolted holds. Down, to where *she* was.

Fari had been speaking to him as they pursued the slaving ships. They were deeply linked when Ki felt *her* call. His brother had shared his deep shock and pleasure at the sudden connection, and the knowledge that went with it. Ki had probed back immediately, deepening the psi-bond.

Wherever Ki's mate had been, she was in ecstasy and thinking only of her lover-to-be.

In those few seconds, Ki became a believer in the magic of *shanna*. From the moment he brushed the thoughts of his soul's mate, he could think of nothing but her. Fari was leading the main attack because Ki's actions were of a single purpose: finding and retrieving his *shanna* from the slaver's stinking grip.

She had been so relaxed when she touched his mind, so happy and satisfied in her fantasy of him. Now, she was terrified and in pain. Someone was using a stick on her, maybe choking her. She might be dying.

If Ki had to slay every OrTan in the galaxy, he would reach her before that happened.

"*Shanna*!" he bellowed, blinded by smoke and gore. "*Dora, shanna. Dora!*"

Strength, my beloved. Strength.

She needed his encouragement. Her life force was slipping away, clawing to hold onto his mind even as he pierced three worthless OrTans with one thrust of his sword.

How could she be so connected to him already? Was she Ardani? Some other type of psi-gifted species?

Ki rounded a corner and found himself facing a row of doors, maybe twenty in all. He knew he was near the ship's center, and these were the Pleasure Rooms, the core of what the OrTan slavers offered—anything a being could desire, for a price. And the slaves held in thrall, some by their own choice, some by obedience collars and pain sticks.

His *shanna* was somewhere in one of those rooms, being tortured. The OrTans had stolen her from her home, kidnapped her into bondage and forced who knows what upon her.

How long had she been a prisoner?

He kicked open the first door.

A blue Coscan woman screamed, covering her single gigantic breast. The furry Denovan who had been suckling it fell backward.

Ki snorted in frustration. "Get to the decks if you desire rescue," he told the Coscan. "My priest will remove your collar and take you home."

The woman gave Ki a grateful smile while the Denovan grabbed his hairy staff and began relieving his own prick. He would cause the woman no problem, Ki knew. Denovans were by nature gentle and passive, though they had terrible trouble finding the interspecies mates they desired. Most humanoids could not tolerate their rotten egg smell.

Ki turned to the next door and broke it down with one thrust of his boot. It was empty.

Roaring with the agony his bride-to-be was transmitting, Ki used his shoulder to batter down the third door. Five tiny Nostans stood against the back wall, huddled around a statuesque Bandu woman wearing the obedience collar.

"Topside," Ki instructed, battling his urge to move on before he ensured the safety of his rescue.

The purple Bandu made a graceful bow. Baring her teeth, she ripped off her collar, screaming with pain and triumph since she realized no OrTans with sticks would appear to get her back in line. As the collar skittered across the floor, the Bandu picked up one of the Nostans and used him to flatten his companions. Ki knew this one would be fine. No species in its right mind would challenge an unfettered Bandu, for obvious reasons.

Door after door, he found rescues or vacancy. With each fruitless kick, he grew more desperate. His *shanna* had faded to nothing but a sliver of light in his mind.

And then he kicked open the last barrier to find none other than Lord Gith, the Vice-Emperor of OrTa. Galactic law prevented Ki from slaying the royalty of another culture, even during rescues.

But Gith was holding Ki's mate by her neck, as if she were nothing more than a child's plaything.

Galactic law suddenly seemed less important.

The shock of seeing his soul's mate, of being near her real, physical body for the first time, nearly drove Ki over the edge. His *pa*-mark fairly crackled, making his muscles flex and flex again. She was perfect, every splendid inch of her. Not Ardani, no. A primitive, likely from the planet called Earth. Naked and vulnerable—and in terrible danger. Who knew what the OrTan trash had done to her?

Roaring like the wild Ardani of old, Ki stormed into the room.

Gith dropped Ki's unconscious prize, then snatched her up again, using her for a shield. His pain stick hovered like a snake beside her neck, and Ki knew if he made the OrTan flinch, the woman would suffer unspeakable agony.

He bared his teeth at the thought, and a low growl rose from his throat. Ki's mind was spinning so violently he could barely focus—yet Gith's hateful face hovered ever-present in his field of vision.

The OrTan's eyes went wide as he recognized the Ardani mating fervor.

"Unhand her," Ki snarled. He swept his diamond blade back and forth, mimicking the many ways he planned to slice Lord Gith, Vice-Emperor or no.

"Or what? You cannot kill me without facing your own death sentence." Gith wrapped a scaly arm around his captive's already-bruised throat. "I have as much right as you to claim my mate. This wench is already mine!"

The OrTan's assertion that he had bedded the woman made Ki's gut roil. If OrTan royalty had hunted, wenched, and laid first claim to this female—no.

No!

He would kill Gith and have done with it, laws and treaties be damned. Nothing would keep him from his soul's mate now that she was within his grasp. The Council might banish him or put him to death, but at that moment, Ki Tul'Mar could have cared less.

Gith lurched sideways, dragging the woman with him. She roused, whimpered, and began a feeble struggle only a finger's length from the double-crescent end of Gith's stick.

Ki bit back a howl and steadied his blade while the OrTan's eyes darted left and right, searching for escape. His grip on Ki's prize loosened, as did his grip on his own thoughts.

Ki's lips curled as Gith's thoughts leaked like spilled water.

The OrTan had been lying.

He hadn't touched the woman, except to kidnap her and attempt to kill her. That claim was no claim at all, by any stretch of galactic law. A fierce swell of triumph caused Ki to snarl again, but not because the law was now on his side.

Because the woman he desired was fully and completely his for the taking. He eased forward, bringing his diamond blade up, then drawing it back to ready position.

Gith jerked his pain stick under the woman's chin, almost touching her flesh. "Stay back, or I will kill her."

"And then I will cut you." Ki's senses were on high. Every movement, every color or sound seemed like a scream. "One scale at a time. And feed your organs to fergilla beasts."

If only he could get a clear field, just for a moment.

Gith seemed to ponder Ki's threat, and the two men circled each other. Ki's *shanna* was always between them.

Tentatively, the Sailmaster reached out toward his beloved's mind, much as he spoke to the sails on his frigate. Psi connections were a tricky thing before mating, especially with a primitive female, one who possessed no direct connection to *pa*—but this splendid woman had reached him once before. Maybe...

Shanna. Shanna!

Her eyelids fluttered, then opened.

"Orion," she murmured.

Ki felt both a thrill at the sweetness of her voice, and puzzlement. Orion must be some primal term of endearment.

Shanna, he psi-whispered, confident that the OrTan collar would translate for him. *The OrTan beast holding you captive—he is attempting to claim you. To assert you have already shared his bed.*

His beloved's enraged expression excited him.

I claim you, too, in the name of all that is right beneath the stars. Ki's *pa*-mark sizzled as he asserted his thoughts. *But you must agree. You must choose me out loud, for all to hear.*

For a moment, the woman hesitated. Her eyes shifted from Gith to Ki, and Ki caught a snatch of her thoughts.

...between the devil and the deep blue sea...

He frowned. It must be some sort of oath.

"What are you doing?" Gith pulled the woman closer. "Are you so bold as to mind-speak to my claimed mate?"

Ki's *shanna*—Elise. Her name was Elise. Ki read it in her thoughts. The sound was so unusual that it almost distracted him even as she made gagging noises at the thought of mating with Gith.

Say it, my beloved. Choose me. Free me to rescue you!

"I—uh." She pulled back and made eye contact with Gith. "Thanks for the ride, but I've never touched you by choice, and don't care to. I choose him. That god-guy, right over there."

Gith's hiss of fury was instant. He shoved Elise away from him and raised his stick to strike her.

Ki lunged forward with his blade and pierced the beast at his shoulder, flipping him away from Elise like a fish on a gig. Gith's pain stick clattered on the floor.

Elise stooped, grabbed it, and whirled around to face Gith even as the OrTan smashed at Ki's diamond blade and tried to grab the warrior to free himself.

"Leave him alone," she yelled, surprising both combatants, who momentarily froze.

Ki gave her a hungry, appreciative stare. By the stars, she was fighting for her own freedom. And for his well-being, too. His *shanna* had a warrior's heart.

How unusual. How exciting.

Lorelei, his mind whispered, and he found himself grinning. The mating fervor nearly overtook him, but Gith staggered back and looked like he might charge her.

Elise raised the stick. "Try it, you scum. I'll cook your stupid green nuts!"

The collar clearly translated her meaning, because Gith's hand dropped to protect whatever type of family jewels he might have.

Ki moved in then, crowding Gith, herding him toward the door with deep swipes of his diamond blade. The OrTan's scales made wet sounds on the stone floor as he inched around the edge of the room. His lizard-like eyes kept flicking to Elise, looking half-furious and half-aroused, and for one long moment, Ki considered killing the fergilla for his impudence.

His conscience fought with him, insisting his murderous urges were the mating fervor talking. Lord Gith was far from worth the trouble his slaying would cause. For now, Elise was the only thing that mattered.

"You will regret this," Gith growled as he dodged through the portal and into the smoking hallway. "I will go to the Council!"

"Then go, while your legs are still attached." Ki thrust his blade toward Gith's scaly thighs. The monster screamed as the diamond blade came within inches of his prick, then shot Ki an angry look before fleeing farther into the passageway.

From behind Ki, Elise whimpered and dropped the pain stick. A soft thump let him know that she had fainted.

Ki lost all thought of Gith, and all reason. He turned quickly, ripped off his tunic, knelt, and wrapped his vulnerable *shanna* in its soft, white cloth. She was murmuring and thrashing as he scooped her from the filthy skull floor and held her tight against his chest.

"You are safe, beloved," he whispered into her golden hair. She smelled of strange flowers and places he had never seen. "I will guard you with my last breath."

At that, his *shanna* relaxed and drifted to sleep, but not before she called him Orion again.

Chapter 3

When Elise woke, she knew she wasn't in a pleasure bed made of air. She was in someone's powerful arms.

Orion!

The man who had saved her from the mange-lizard had her cradled against his naked chest, and she was wearing his shirt. It smelled almost leathery-like, with heavy, sweet spices. He was striding through fire, ignoring the smoke and heat and people screaming, like he did this hero stuff every day.

Elise caught glimpses of other men like Orion, battling with swords that seemed to be made out of diamonds, or rubies, or sapphires. Each blade had a slightly different color, which seemed to change as the warrior swung the weapon. Alligator creeps dropped like ugly green flies. Naked people of all shapes and hues ran past, headed in the same direction as Orion. Up, up, up, and out a large portal into a glowing darkness.

Darkness couldn't glow, of course.

But this darkness did.

Holding tight to her savior, Elise peered around his muscled arm and caught her breath.

They were floating in outer space!

No, no. Wait. They were on a ship with a black deck.

And now they were on something like a gangplank, crossing over to—

"Oh, my." Elise's eyes widened.

The silver pirate's ship she had been dreaming about waited for her like a ghost frigate. It looked like something out of *Peter Pan* or *Brigadoon*. Massive silver sails rippled against the endless constellations, and ropes and riggings twinkled in the ethereal black-glow. There were at least fifty men working cranks and wheels, and each of them looked up as Orion carried her onto the ship's shiny deck.

Elise was shocked, overly aware of her barely clothed state, yet too excited to focus on her humiliation. *I swear, the sails and the wood – they look like they're made of stardust. And the stardust seems…it feels…alive. It's almost like I can hear it, whispering.*

She should have been cold on a ship's deck in outer space. Freezing, even. And she shouldn't have been able to breathe. Her skin was warm, though, and her breath came easily.

Do not be afraid, murmured a strong voice in her mind, and she knew it was Orion.

My name is not Orion, beloved. It is Ki Tul'Mar, Sailmaster of Arda. Though if Orion is a term of endearment, I will gladly accept it, along with your attentions.

Elise stiffened in the pirate's arms.

Her attentions? What did that mean?

Did this guy think that just because he rescued her from the alligator freaks, he could fuck her?

Laughter floated through her brain. There was a heat behind it, yet it was gentle, like an intimate tickle. *Yes. Of course I will.*

"Like hell!" Elise smacked at his rock-hard shoulder. "Put me down."

Ki Tul'Mar laughed at her again, this time out loud.

"Put me down, you jerk!" Elise hit him again, though she was half afraid he'd drop her into nothingness and she would float away like some half-naked balloon.

We have inertial dampening, and an atmospheric shield. It surrounds the ship, beloved. You would not float away.

"Then...put...me...down." Elise's anger iced her words, but the pirate or king or Sailmaster or whatever he was paid her no more mind than if she were a child throwing a tantrum.

"In good time," he said, and the rich timbre of his voice made Elise shiver.

Arrogant bastard. And I hope you read that thought, buddy. Stay out of my head. Got me?

There was no answer, so Elise assumed the big bully grasped her message. Still highly annoyed, she struggled against his grip, but Ki Tul'Mar only shifted her until she was seated in his arms. She felt the hot grip of his hands on her ass, kneading. Touching her in an intimate, possessive way, in front of people.

Even as she pushed against his chest, the incredible firmness of his muscles made her mouth go dry. His eyes were so black she thought she might fall into them, and his hair, so long and thick—she wanted to touch it and then trace the perfect line of his strong jaw and dimpled chin. On his chest—oh, my. The strangest tattoo. It was silver and shimmering like the ship's sails, and shaped in intricate flame patterns. Elise reached out to touch it, but Ki caught her hand while still using his spare arm to hold her in check.

"That would not be wise," he rumbled. The husk in his voice was unmistakable. "If you connect with me more completely at this moment, I will lose all restraint."

"Sire," said a man approaching quickly from the left. He was as tall as the warriors now streaming back to the frigate, blades still drawn—but this man had no sword. He was dressed in deep purple robe. There were patterns on his cheek, like a henna tattoo, only made of that same almost-living glitter in the sails and on Ki's chest.

Ki stopped massaging Elise's backside and turned, holding her out so quickly she didn't have time to react.

The robed man passed his hands over her head without touching her and said, "She is unharmed. The simple healing pass should stop any bruising, and the collar has been on but a few stellar hours. Removal will be without risk."

Elise focused on the purple-robe guy. "You can take it off? Without it killing me?"

"Yes, Grace." The man nodded.

"I'm not Grace." Elise smiled. "But take the collar off anyway, please."

"It is a term of respect, my lady. I am Akad, the priest of this vessel, and I would be honored to assist you." The robed man held out his arms to accept her, but Ki held on with a growl. Elise felt his breathing grow rapid, and her skin prickled.

"Sire, I must take her below." Akad sounded patient, but fearful. "Only for a few moments, and you may stay outside the entire time."

"Inside," Ki snarled.

"A-As you wish." Akad shrugged, and Elise realized that most of the triumphant warriors had stopped celebrating to watch this exchange.

"And I will carry her," Ki added.

The implication was clear. No one, not even this painted man in a robe, was to touch her.

God, he is so arrogant!

Elise fumed inwardly as the sea of warriors and deckhands parted for them to enter the first of three main holds. Elise sensed their eyes sweeping over her barely-covered body. Her heart pounded harder at the thought, and she fought a wild urge to let the shirt fall open and see if one of them would rescue her from Ki.

Somehow, she figured that was unlikely.

Akad held the door for Ki, and as he carted Elise into the silvery passageway, she heard Akad whisper to the nearest man, "Fetch Fari. Make haste!"

Ki's giant strides carried Elise so quickly that she couldn't get her bearings. Doors, bays and bins streamed by in a blur. A couple of times, she saw murals. Strange paintings of three wild-looking women, with fangs like small tigers and silver fire on their faces.

The sights, the strange, cloying smells—everything was so new, so bright and overwhelming. "Slow down," she begged, hoping she wouldn't get sick.

Again, Ki ignored her. He made a broad turn, then hauled her into a room full of flat gray tables covered with naked women wearing collars like Elise's. Some of them were touching each other, hugging like frightened children, or long-lost friends. Others were touching each other in a more intimate fashion.

Elise felt a tightening between her own legs as two dark-skinned women nearby toyed with each other's nipples. Beside them, another couple was sinking slowly to the floor. The woman closest to Elise lowered her head between her partner's legs, and the woman being pleasured let out a low groan.

These people know no shame.

The thought shocked her and aroused her all at once. Heat rose to Elise's cheeks, and she looked away—straight into the eyes of the four-breasted woman from the OrTan peepshow. Her blush grew painful. Thankfully, the woman didn't seem to recognize her.

"Do you like to watch others being pleasured, beloved?" Ki's voice was ragged—and maddening.

"No," she snapped, even though she knew she was lying. "And I'm not your beloved. I don't even know you."

"But you will, *shanna*."

Elise rolled her eyes, then decided to get a fix on her surroundings in case escape became a possibility. A few glances told her that she was in this ship's version of a sick bay, and she realized Akad must be some sort of doctor or healer. Waiting for Ki to put her down, she marveled at the array of computer-like instruments, and she wondered at the advancement of their medical science. Judging by the frigate, she guessed Ki's people were light years ahead of Earth in science and technology.

On the wall directly to Elise's right, another strange mural caught her attention. The same three women she had seen in the passageway. One blond, one redhead, and one with—strangely changing hair. Almost iridescent. In this picture, the silver-marked and naked beauties held swords. Their toothy mouths were opened in a group howl, and at their feet lay a dark-headed man. His hands were bound.

Good for them. Elise cut her eyes toward the side of Ki's head and dug her nails into his shoulder.

He didn't respond.

Akad entered quietly, and he motioned for the waiting women to clear a space on the nearest table. One of them frowned and bared vampire-like fangs, but they all moved. Ki strode forward and eased Elise onto the bright surface. It was cool and hard, yet comforting, and it warmed quickly to the temperature of her skin.

When Ki stepped back, Elise had a chance to take her rescuer's full measure. He was easily seven feet tall, and maybe taller. There was no hint of the lankiness typical to men of that height. This one was all muscle, and just as she had dreamed him to be—flowing black hair spilling down across his bare golden shoulders, covering the tips of his silver tattoo. Corded chest, arms that would put a weightlifter to shame, tapered waist, solid hips…oh, man. He was Orion, in the flesh, dressed in flowing black pants, with a sword in a scabbard against his left leg.

There was a distinct bulge beside that sword, and Elise found she couldn't take her eyes off of it.

Was he as well-endowed as the green guy she had seen on the slaving ship?

Not that it matters. Mr. Arrogance isn't getting anywhere near me.

But the intense, ravenous look in Ki's eyes said differently. The man seemed absolutely possessed by desire. Elise simultaneously steamed with rage and a secret, guilty excitement.

Did he want her that badly?

And why was he calling her beloved?

Was he reading her thoughts, even now?

Could he tell she was attracted to him?

Akad slipped into view, approaching slowly with a pair of golden tongs and a small cup. He handed her the cup, which was full of thick, greenish liquid.

"Swallow this, Grace. It will dull the pain when I take your collar."

Elise glanced at the swirling liquid and reverted to her second rule: Trust no one but Georgia. The thought of her cousin brought a surge of emotion, and Elise bit back a shaky sigh. "Um, no. I'm not into alien drugs. Just take the collar off."

Looking flustered, Akad again offered the cup. "Please, Grace. You will need this. If not now," he cut his eyes toward Ki, "then later."

Ki made a low hiss and started to pace. "Make haste, priest."

"Is something wrong with him?" Elise followed Ki's irregular course with her eyes. "He acts almost drunk. And definitely stupid."

"Ardani mating fervor." Akad pressed the cup into Elise's hands. "It happens when a warrior finds his soul's mate, just before the bonding ceremony and the first joining. The more powerful the warrior, the worse the fervor."

Elise definitely didn't like the sound of that. She let the cup rest against her fingers, feeling the warmth of the potion inside. She made eye contact with Akad, who seemed to be trying to avoid her gaze. "What will this do to me?"

"It will lessen the pain of collar removal." Akad glanced at Elise's hands. "And it will relax your muscles for a few stellar hours. No permanent effects. About this, you have the word of an Ardani holy man."

Akad seemed quite serious when he spoke his last sentence, and Elise's instinct kicked in enough to tell her that Akad seemed on the up and up.

She took a swig of the potion.

It tasted like Crème de Menthe, heated, and it made her tongue numb.

Ki paced by, once more fixing her with a hungry stare. The hard-on in his pants seemed larger.

Elise downed the rest of the drink.

Just then, a warrior burst into the sick bay. Save for a few inches in height, he might have been Ki's double. Elise felt a flicker of attraction, then shook it off. It was bad enough finding one arrogant pirate handsome. Two would be unthinkable.

Ki and his double squared off, and almost immediately, a noise began in Elise's mind. Two voices, dueling, louder and louder.

...let her be properly prepared, brother.

Get away from me...

Ki, she is a primitive. Listen to reason...

...go back to pumping fergilla...

The shorter man drew his blade, and Ki drew his in response.

The two men began to duel in earnest, right there in the sick bay. Naked women stumbled and fell away from them, clearing room for their seemingly deadly battle.

Elise gasped, but Akad shook his head. "It is typical, Grace. Fari is only helping to manage the fervor until you are...capable. Now, close your eyes. Once I remove the collar, our speech will make little sense to you—but you will understand soon enough."

Not wanting to obey but feeling strangely compelled, Elise did as the priest asked and let her lids drift shut.

"One more thing," Akad whispered. "Do not be afraid. When an Ardani warrior loves you, he will do nothing you do not desire, and everything you want. You have my word on that as well."

Before she could open her eyes, Elise felt the priest remove her shirt. There was a tug at her neck, a brief flash of pain, and then nothing. The collar was gone.

When she looked around, a few women were grinning at her, running fingers across their own collars. She smiled at them in understanding, then realized she was dizzy.

"I don't feel right," she whispered to Akad.

More warriors had entered the sick bay, and they were restraining Ki, attempting to take him out of the room. His eyes were wide, and he was howling.

Elise's heart twisted at the sight of his desperation. She had a sudden urge to yell at them to leave her beloved alone.

My beloved? Oh, God. I'm drunk.

Akad lifted her from the table. He said something she couldn't understand—it sounded almost like birdsong rather than words.

Ki's shorter double took her from Akad. Fari. Yes, that was his name. He was Ki's brother, and he was gentle as he carried her out of the sickbay and back down the long hallway.

It was somewhere in between the hold exit and the main deck that Elise realized she was completely naked. She tensed, but only a little. The tongue-numbing drink was doing its job.

Warm air passed over every inch of her, bringing her nipples to attention. All over the frigate, deck hands and warriors stared at her with covetous desire. She could only hope Fari hurried to wherever they were going, but he didn't. He walked slowly, as if he were part of some procession, until he reached the tallest point of the frigate's main deck.

With Akad beside him and Ki nearby—but held by six different warriors—Fari raised Elise up, then forward, like he might drop her into the ravenous crowd of men below.

Some part of her mind wanted to fight, to protest, but she couldn't muster the muscle tension.

"*Elise!*" Fari bellowed. "*Shanna! Ki Tul'Mar!*"

Ki roared his assent and struggled with his captors.

Akad echoed Fari's words, adding more phrases Elise didn't understand—but she had the distinct impression she was being married in some bizarre alien way.

It's okay. No problem. I can do this. Whatever it takes to get home, to get back to my cousin.

The crowd below her roared three times, in quick succession, and Ki was led away.

Fari made an agonizingly slow turn, showing Elise's every angle and inch to the cheering men.

She tried to find her embarrassment, but it simply wasn't there.

An Ardani warrior will do nothing you do not desire...everything you want...

The priest's words ran through her mind.

So, did she desire being on display?

Of course not.

But…there was an undeniable ache between her legs as the men looked her over. Desiring her, but not daring to touch her. Because she belonged to their Sailmaster. Because she was the Sailmaster's woman, forever out of reach but delicious to dream of fucking every night, while they searched for their own mates.

Where did that come from? What the hell am I thinking?

Some of the men were gripping themselves, in obvious pain.

For a second, there on that space frigate, drugged and naked in the arms of a complete stranger, on display for a crew full of pirates, Elise Ashton felt more powerful than ever before.

And more excited.

Fari held her suspended for a few more seconds, then turned, marched forward into a ship cabin, and placed her gently on her feet.

Elise swayed as her heavy lids lifted to take in the huge room. It was bigger than most Earth houses. The furnishings were sparse, only a desk and a large table with chairs. On the right wall, Elise saw another mural with the three vampire girls, this time fighting each other with swords…and in the very back of the room, a large curtained bed.

Candles were ablaze on the floor, on the table, on virtually every flat surface. The light scent of honey and lemon wafted through the air, and the effect of the flames on the silvery floor was hypnotic.

This is the Sailmaster's cabin, Elise's fuzzy mind told her.

And the Sailmaster was indeed waiting, in the back, beside the bed. No handlers were in sight, and Ki was naked. He had a hard-on that would put the green man on the OrTan ship to shame, and his face was slack.

Elise quickly realized that Ki Tul'Mar had been drugged, too.

Thank God.

And then Fari closed and locked the cabin door—without leaving.

Elise's eyes came fully open now.

"Oh, no. Sorry," she slurred. "I might—with him, maybe—and I'm not even sure about that, but absolutely not with you, too—"

But before she could finish, Fari once more lifted her and carried her straight back to the bed, back to the waiting Ki, who was growling again, in a low, spine-stirring way.

"I can't do this," Elise muttered, but she sounded half-hearted, even to herself. Her drugged brain and body acknowledged what her pride didn't want to admit—how very much she wanted to experience every sexy inch of Ki.

Fari lowered Elise to the bed and stepped back, making way for his brother's approach.

Ki stumbled forward and came to a halt inches from the bed. His eyes swept up and down Elise's body, consuming her with the fire of his desire. His need was so obvious and desperate, so raw and real, that any thought she had of fighting him vanished on the spot.

But, Fari...

Ki's brother was still standing on the far side of the bed, seemingly ignoring them. Elise's head was spinning. She stretched out, trying to ignore him, too.

The sheets felt soft on her naked skin, and the dancing candlelight and warm fragrances washed over her.

Ki lowered himself into the bed beside her. He smelled of leather and sweat and desire, like warrior's musk. Elise took long breaths, enjoying the sheer maleness of his scent, the absolute perfection of his hard, warm flesh pressing the length of her body. His silver tattoo was hot and damp, like tongues against her chest.

A rustle of cloth caught Elise's attention, and she realized Fari had closed the bed curtain on his side. One by one, all of the curtains closed. And then Elise heard the cabin door open, then close, the lock once more clicking into place.

She was alone with Ki.

Relief swept her, followed quickly by fear.

This was a seven-foot alien stranger, and she was alone with him. At his mercy.

But she wasn't afraid. Far from it. In fact, she was more aroused than she had ever been. Wet and aching, her body screamed for Ki's hands, for his mouth, for the stiff cock she could feel against her like a hot piece of iron.

Ki was speaking in her mind, whispering, but she couldn't completely understand him. Without the collar, she was fishing for words and sounds that made sense, learning as she went. And so was Ki, but his learning was strictly tactile.

Here? His fingers seemed to ask as they brushed her cheek.

Here? They inquired as they crept over her neck, as powerful as vises but as gentle as feathers.

And then his lips were on hers, pressing hard as he cupped her head, until she groaned with the pleasure of finally joining with him in some small way.

All those nights, waiting.

All those nights, dreaming.

Ki was pushing gently into her mouth, tasting her like a starving man might sample the first course of a banquet. His tongue was rough and soft at the same time, thrilling her as it met her own in a slow dance of excitement. He pulled back to kiss her cheeks, her chin, her neck.

Elise bowed against the pillows, wondering what his teeth would feel like on her skin. As if in answer, he nibbled the flesh beneath her ear and down, toward her collarbone, and back up again on the other side.

She felt connected to him, and completely without fear. Her thoughts seemed to guide his touches, and his throaty growls made her shiver all over.

"I wish I could still understand you," she whispered.

Ki took her nipple into his mouth and sucked, speaking a universal language.

Elise moaned, arching her back as his hands slipped behind her, pulling her close. Biting and teasing with his tongue, he made her slit ache for his cock. She wrapped her fingers in his long, soft hair and pressed his face closer.

Sighing, he changed nipples, this time starting harder and faster.

Elise's pussy was so wet she didn't know how much more she could stand.

Sensing her crazed arousal, Ki let one hand stray down her hip, stroking the sensitive slit between her thighs, then slipping farther into her pool of excitement.

Elise bucked as he slid his fingers higher and higher, until he found her clit and pressed against it.

"Please," she whispered as he made slow circles against her swollen bud, keeping easy rhythm with her hips.

Ki pulled back and looked at her, still using his hand to push her closer and closer to ecstasy. His lids were heavy, but his eyes were bright and fevered. The man was splendid in his nakedness as he lounged there, staring at her, fingering her clit until she came with a loud cry of surprise and joy. And then he kept going, this time dipping his fingers inside her pussy, suddenly, almost rough, but not too rough. First one finger, then two, then three.

Elise couldn't help herself. She spread her legs wide, giving him full access to do as he pleased.

Grinning that insufferably arrogant grin, Ki left his fingers in place, pushing in and out of her sweet recesses, deeper and deeper. Then he leaned down and ran his tongue from his knuckles to the apex of Elise's wet flesh. She groaned at the sweet feel of his mouth as he teased, drawing out her excitement as he flicked against her clit again and again.

Elise's arousal blended with her drugged haze, and she lost count of her orgasms as Ki worked his lips and tongue up and down her swollen slit. Her insides were aching, wanting more of him, all of him, yet even so relaxed and ready, she feared being able to take his full, incredible cock.

He raised his head, as if tracking her thoughts. "Do not be afraid," he whispered, and Elise's eyes flew open all the way.

"I understood you," she said, surprised by the thick huskiness of her voice.

Ki said something else, but this time, Elise couldn't grasp it.

He sighed. "Time, beloved. Time. Until…show. Show."

Elise frowned, and then she grasped what Ki was trying to say—what Akad had said before. *For a time, our speech will make little sense to you—but you will understand soon enough.*

The mental connection she was making with Ki, *with her mate*, would eventually let her know Ardani language with no collar, and it would allow Ki to comprehend her words, too.

Until then, she would have to show him what she feared—and what she wanted.

Elise felt her lips curl in a smile not unlike Ki's hungry snarl.

If he wanted showing, that much she could do.

The calming drug had full hold of Ki, and still his blood roared. His *pa*-mark pulsed like a thing possessed. He felt wild, yet he kept himself in check easily, thanks to Akad's masterful potions.

Ki had no idea it would feel like this, lying with his *shanna*, touching her and tasting her. Joining with her, mind and soul. Even though her primitive physiology prevented them from establishing the full psychic joining Ardani couples practiced, what he had with Elise was enough. More than enough.

And now she was looking at him the way he had first looked at her, as if she could eat him whole.

He leaned back, taking in the sight of her, from her kiss-swollen lips and nipples to the golden patch of wet hair between her legs. Her quim was so warm, so moist and tight. His mast throbbed with the force of his passion, and he wanted nothing more than to sail into her.

When she was ready. When she wanted him, and not before.

No matter how fierce his passion, he would not take his mate by force, or cause her pain.

Elise pushed herself up in their bed and leaned toward him, meeting his lips. She kissed him deeply, sharing her mouth and tongue as only a mate does. Ki's hands gripped the bedclothes. If not for the calming drug, he would lose all control this first time. This woman was almost too much for him.

And now her kisses were moving down to his throat, to his smooth, hard chest. She flicked across his *pa*-mark, sending shocks through his muscles. He gasped, as did she. Her eyes widened as she touched the mark again, this time with her fingertips.

She was sensing it, the power of his mark. His small piece of the universe's living force. He couldn't yet explain it to her, but later, from her lessons, she would understand.

Tracing the line of his mark with her tongue until she captured his nipples, Elise seemed to be taking his *pa*-mark in stride for now. And sweet fates, but she was an expert with her mouth, her tongue. His cock was fairly pounding between his legs, and still her kisses moved lower, to his belly, and lower, into the thick patch of hair surrounding his manhood.

There, she stopped and pulled back. He could read the desire in her eyes, feel it in her thoughts, but also her fear.

Ardani males were much larger than Earth males, in every way. Ki was both proud of this, and worried.

Would their coupling hurt his *shanna*?

Elise's fingers teased the curled hair around his cock, and then she gripped him, wrapping her fingers around his thickness.

Ki threw his head back and groaned. Her touch was almost enough to override the drugs and send him into a rutting frenzy. He had to hold on, let her find her way and show him what she could take.

Elise seemed more fascinated than shy, and her innocent, hungry expression touched Ki's heart. No doubt she had known some Earth lovers, but she was naïve to Ardani ways. So many surprises lay in store for her, and so much freedom. As much or as little as she wanted.

Right now, her lips wanted to push him close to insanity.

She had lowered her head, and she was kissing his mast, slowly, working her tongue from stem to stern. Her fingers cupped the tender sack at its base, and Ki groaned again. He felt Elise's thoughts joining more fully with his, reading his desires, his fantasies. He closed his eyes as she took his cock in her mouth, as much as she could hold, moving up and down, giving him a hint of the pleasures awaiting him between her legs.

Time and again, Elise brought him to the edge of orgasm with her mouth, then stopped, letting him cool down. His teeth ground together, and when he couldn't take another second, he sat up, pulling her to him.

He kissed her, fighting not to squeeze her too hard.

Wordless, his *shanna* pulled back. She lifted herself off the bed and straddled him, and he felt her wetness on the tip of his cock.

Grinding his teeth so hard his jaws hurt, Ki let her lower herself slowly onto him. He heard her gasping, felt the soft brush of her breasts on his face, and then she was eye to eye with him.

Her mouth was open, and she was breathing hard. Her thoughts and feelings conveyed pleasure and pain, but more than anything, desire. The feel of being inside her quim undid Ki completely, and he lifted her up, bringing her down once, then twice. She didn't flinch. Instead, her slit seemed to open wide, growing wetter and more welcoming.

"Yes," she whispered, closing her eyes. "I can do this. Yes. I want you. All of you."

Though he couldn't understand her words in full, Ki knew he had the invitation he had been waiting for. Quickly but gently, he lifted his *shanna* again, this time easing her onto her back and settling between her legs.

His first thrust was paradise. She groaned, but her thoughts told him it was from sheer pleasure. Elise's eyes were closed, and she had her hands on her own nipples. The sight drove Ki to new levels of arousal, and he thrust into her again.

Elise's hips rolled to meet him.

She was pinching her nipples now, her head turning slowly back and forth. Ki sensed her wish for him to give her more, faster, and he did.

The calming drug was wearing off, and he felt like his skin and *pa* were on fire. She fit his cock like a soft scabbard, and he knew he couldn't hold back another moment.

Elise sensed his urgency. Her hands left her breasts and grabbed his arms, digging her nails into his flesh as she lifted herself to meet him harder and harder.

Ki growled, pounding into her quim, hearing the wet sound of their sex, the loud screams of delight from his beloved. She wrapped her legs around him, holding him possessively inside her as he hammered her over and over, deeper and deeper. All sensation revolved around his *shanna*. All life, all breath, all pleasure.

Elise cried out as she climaxed, and Ki howled as he exploded within her, draining his seed until not a drop remained.

And still, his *shanna* kept her legs tightly wrapped. She didn't seem to want to let him go.

All is as it should be, he thought as stupor settled over him. How was it that he had done without this feeling his entire life? Had he really believed he didn't want a soul's mate?

Elise stirred beneath him, and he rolled to his side, still cradling her. This was bliss. She was bliss. Ki allowed his thoughts to flow toward Fari, to let his brother taste of his deep satisfaction.

Finally. By the worlds, finally. So long as the OrTan scum-prince does not convince the Council of his viewpoint, all will be well, indeed.

Chapter 4

Hours later, Elise stroked Ki's long black hair. His forehead was damp, and his sleep-breathing was rhythmic and peaceful. He was holding her like a long-lost treasure, and she didn't know what to make of that. She didn't know what to make of anything that happened in the last day and a half.

There, wrapped in the protective curtains of a giant bed, with a sleeping giant in her arms, Elise could almost convince herself she was back on Earth. Maybe having a fling with some eccentric millionaire who had left her pussy sweetly sore and thoroughly satisfied.

And yet, this man was an alien. A warrior. He was so wild and fierce that a priest had to drug them both to keep her from being wounded on her wedding night.

Sweet Heaven. By these people's standards, I'm married to this god.

The effects of the drug Akad had given her were wearing off, and her thoughts were clear. Still, try as she might, Elise couldn't stretch her mind around being this stranger's wife. His soul's mate.

But they had spoken mind to mind, body to body. They had shared an intimacy that Elise had never known. She had intended to do whatever it took to get home, and she had just spent hours having wild sex with an alien. And he seemed so...so...sweet. Like someone she didn't want to leave.

Surely he was too good to be true.

"Rule one," she murmured. "In the end, all men are boring."

Who was she kidding? How could this—*warrior* ever be boring?

"Rule Two." Elise heard the quiver in her voice. "Trust no one but Georgia."

Ki stirred in her arms and sighed. Elise teared up, thinking about her cousin, wishing she could tell her about all the incredible things that had happened.

Sensing her distress, Ki's obsidian eyes opened. They were soft and liquid from sleep, and before she formed a full thought, Elise kissed one, then the other.

Ki raised up on one elbow, tracing the outline of her cheek. "What is hurting you, beloved?"

"I understood you." Elise smiled.

"It should be less trouble, with the first mating behind us."

Elise thought about commenting on his arrogance in assuming there would be a second mating, but she didn't bother. This man could fuck her any time.

Ki leaned forward and kissed her. His lips felt like hot silk, claiming hers, and her heart started to beat faster even as he pulled back.

"I asked you what brought you tears while I was sleeping," he murmured.

His gaze was so intense and serious that Elise felt unsettled. His medication had worn off, too. What if he had a temper?

"I do," he said matter-of-factly. "But I would never harm you."

Elise squirmed, avoiding Ki's next kiss. "Do you read my thoughts all the time?"

He shrugged one muscled shoulder. "When you broadcast them. In time, I will read them all, yes. And you will share mine as well. We will both want that."

"Oh, we will?" Elise stiffened. "You assume a lot."

Ki grinned, pulling her to him, under him. He kissed her deeply, letting his tongue caress hers, moving one large hand over her naked skin until she groaned.

If that was his way of diffusing *her* temper, it was very effective. His fingers and his silver tattoo sang to her body, and her body answered with gasps and shudders.

When his mouth fastened on her nipple, Elise stopped thinking clearly. All she could feel was the fire of his mouth, the exquisite pleasure of each nibble and suck. His thoughts drifted through her mind, and she saw through his sensations how soft she was, how she tasted, how much her responsive body excited him.

Heat rose to her cheeks.

She had never known herself like that, through a lover's eyes.

Then you have never known a lover, Ki whispered in her mind.

His thoughts grew more open, and she could literally see herself—her wet, swollen nipples, the soft red marks here and there from their previous lovemaking, and her curves, which Ki explored with his sizzling tongue for long, agonizing minutes.

Elise could smell the powdery scent of her own skin, feel its softness in his mouth, and when he slid his fingers deep into her wetness, she could feel her own heat.

Ki's touches were growing firmer, and Elise was bonded to his arousal. Wild tides coursed through her as he pulled back and seared her with his dark, possessive gaze. His fingers stayed busy, thrusting in and out of her pussy, getting her ready for his already-throbbing cock.

You are mine, shanna. Never think to leave me.

Elise could barely concentrate as he spread her legs. She was lost in her own excitement and his feral desire, and she wanted him inside her, now. Images flashed through her mind, fantasies of the many ways he could take her—and she didn't know if they were his thoughts or hers. She didn't even care.

Rumbling his arousal, Ki turned her over and drew her up on all-fours. Grasping her ass with both of his strong hands, he pumped his cock into her wet pussy, sinking to the hilt and drawing a moan of pleasure from her parted lips.

"You are perfect," he said aloud, easing out, then slamming into her again.

Elise felt her breasts jiggle with the impact, and then Ki's hands closed over them, pinching her nipples gently and letting go. She moaned again, louder, completely wrapped in the dual sensation of his pleasure and her own.

Once more, Ki slid almost completely out of her, and she whimpered.

"Do you want all of me?" he rasped.

"Yes. Damn you. Yes!" Elise dug her fingers into the sheets, pushing back toward him until he drove into her slit again. Squeezing her legs together, she held him inside, surprising him, arousing him even more. His thrusts became harder and faster.

"Don't hold back," Elise ordered. "Give me everything."

Ki's answer was a growl, and a thrust so deep Elise thought he must have filled her entire insides.

She felt herself expanding to hold him, again and again. There was no more pain, only pleasure. Only the most deep and satisfying penetration she could imagine. He packed every inch of her, his sack slapping against her swollen folds. She heard it through his ears and her own. The smell of their lovemaking rose like smoke from the ever-burning candles, sweet and salty all at once.

"Fuck me!" Elise demanded, wondering if she could have enough of his thick, hard cock.

Ki gripped her hips and rammed into her pussy, rocking them both back and forth so hard the bed shook.

Elise came with a bone-shattering scream, followed quickly by Ki's untamed howl as he emptied himself in her wide-open slit.

Aftershocks rattled Elise as Ki threw his arms around her, cupped her breasts, and pulled her against his chest—all the while leaving himself inside her. Her nipples beaded and ached beneath his tender touch, and once more, he said, "Never leave me."

This time, the arrogance was gone from Ki's voice. His words sounded more like a statement of love, or a plea.

For a moment, Elise wondered at all she didn't know about Ardani customs. Was she allowed to come and go, if she so chose? Or was she just a glorified prisoner? These things she would have to ask Ki, along with how she might contact Georgia, or bring her cousin for a visit.

But later.

When he wasn't biting her neck like that.

* * * * *

Seven stellar days had passed, and Ki's new-mating time was nearly finished. He did not want it to end, even though he knew *Astoria* and the crew needed his attention. He had felt battle docking at least three times, but he had ignored the horns. His mast had been full inside his mate's quim, and her heat was all-consuming.

Still, he could not keep her to himself forever. There were her lessons with Akad to be completed, and her Presentation to the court and people of Arda—the official satisfaction of the Law of Keeping. The sooner those things were done, the better. Ki could go back to speaking to the *pa* in his sails, hunting slavers and rogues, and plumbing the sweet depths of his *shanna*.

How he would bear being separated from her, even for brief rescue campaigns, he couldn't imagine.

This precious period of being totally alone, with only the intrusion of galley hands slipping food inside the door—it would never be repeated, though Ki had already vowed to himself that he would spend a lifetime trying.

Ardani lived a very long time, even by galactic standards. Now that they were mated, Elise would share his lifespan. They would have Earth centuries to know each other, and to steal long periods alone, with only food from servants to distract them.

His *shanna* was more exciting and intelligent than even he could have imagined. She understood the concept of *pa*, which was the living quicksilver of the universe. She knew that *pa* suffused Ardani flesh and sailcraft, and formed the basis of their society. He had already taught Elise basic *Kon'pa* steps, which they performed each morning, together, chest to chest and leg to leg, inside the sacred ring of candles. Often they finished with a slow coupling, never disturbing the circle.

Ki could not get enough of Elise. He was alternately aching and exhausted, starved and fulfilled, but he was loathe to close his eyes. He wanted the exhaustion. He wanted to be in his beloved's quim every stellar minute, driving toward her very core, making her more his own with each thrust of his cock.

He longed to watch her sweet face as she climaxed. He wanted to run his lips over her salty skin. He lived to bathe her in warm water, soaping her with sweetleaves and Andromedan spices, as he had only this morning. She was his and loving it, demanding that he take her in every possible position, in every possible way.

Sometimes she called him by his name. Sometimes she called him a bastard, with her hands wrapped in his hair, forcing his face closer, pleading with him to finish what his tongue had started.

At the moment, she was draped across him, still damp from their bath, and wet from their lovemaking. She was sleeping, but he had his fingers inside her quim, slipping in and out, tracing the soft, velvet outline of her sex.

Could anything be more pleasurable than touching this woman?

Brother. Fari's psi voice was soft and tentative, more a sigh than a call. Ki knew his brother had entered the cabin, and that Fari was sharing in some of Ki's besotted feelings as the Sailmaster slowly made love to Elise.

This was not troubling to Ki. No doubt Fari had been driven near to distraction during the new-mating time. It was common for brothers or close family members to share in the pleasures of their relative's mates—but somehow, Ki suspected Elise would not be gratified to know this. If Elise had been Ardani, Fari might well have spent some of the week with them, maximizing pleasure for all.

As it was, both Ki and Fari had feared Ki's warrior woman might unman Fari if he so much as insinuated this possibility. And so, in moments of ultimate climax, Ki had shared what he could with his brother. He was not a selfish man, and no matter his urges to pitch Fari overboard, he wouldn't have denied his sibling such small gratifications. Besides, if Ki were slain in battle, it would be up to Fari to see to Elise's needs.

All of her needs.

She had married his living family, his brother Fari and sister Krysta alike. And when Fari and Krysta married, their mates, too, would be bound to Ki and Elise.

Ki sighed.

Perhaps Akad would explain all of that to Elise in some acceptable fashion, during her first lesson today.

Elise groaned and rolled beneath him as his fingers found her slippery clit and toyed with it.

"I want you in my pussy," she murmured, more asleep than awake. "Please. I want you so much."

Acutely aware of Fari's silent presence nearby, Ki rolled forward, easing Elise back on the pillows.

"Now." She sighed, opening her legs. "Now, Ki."

From somewhere near the main table, Fari groaned, but Elise didn't notice.

Ki's *pa* was alive with his brother's nearness, with Elise's thick musk, and with his own overpowering arousal. Elise connected with his thoughts as he thrust into her quim, driving hard, as far as he could go. She moaned with pleasure, with her total acceptance of his body and all that he could offer. He stroked again and again, bringing her to a frenzy, then slowed, stopped, and pulled out.

"Bastard." She groaned and slapped his shoulders.

He leaned down and suckled her nipples, gently at first, then with more and more pressure. Her hands pressed on his head as he curled down, tasting her wetness. Her body shuddered, and he rose up once more and drove into her slit with the force of his passion. She cried out, gripping his hips with her legs. In and out, in and out—by the heavens, there could be nothing so sweet.

Elise groaned.

Ki and Fari groaned almost at the same moment, and then his *shanna* trembled with her forceful release. Her bucking and cries of pleasure brought Ki's explosion soon after, and he knew Fari had also been relieved—though not so completely.

Too late, Ki realized some of this thought had trickled to his beloved.

"Ki." Elise's nails dug into his shoulders as he gently left the warmth of her sex. "Ki! Your brother's in the room!"

Her tone conveyed shock and horror, even dismay.

Fari hesitated, but on Ki's psi command, came to the bed, entering the curtains on the opposite side from Ki. He was still clothed, though his breeches and tunic bore the stain of his arousal and release.

"I meant no disrespect," Fari said in a husky voice. "Out of honor for your culture, I scarcely intruded on your first-mating time—but it has been torture, Elise."

Elise had claws full into Ki's flesh. "What is he talking about? I don't—this isn't—Ki!"

Ki cradled Elise, certain he was bleeding on the sheets from her panicked nail-stabbings. "Our ways are different from yours, *shanna*. It is the mind-talking, the *pa* we share. Everything flows like water between siblings, and my brother and sister—"

"Sister?" Elise sat straight up and pushed Ki back, giving Fari an agonizing view of her nakedness. "There's been a sister knowing all this, too?"

"Not all," murmured Fari. "She is back home, on Arda. But no doubt she has tasted some of Ki's immense joy. One would have to be psi-blind to ignore it."

Elise shot Ki a look of humiliated betrayal. She gathered the little-used sheet to her, covering most of her tantalizing freckles and curves. Her thoughts were of love and sharing, and Ki's heart ached as he understood her belief—that if he was willing to share her with anyone else, he did not love her as she had come to love him.

She felt less than, exposed, and—the word was difficult, but it was akin to "bargain." Cheap. At lower cost. The concept confused him, but he thought he understood.

"I love you, *shanna*. I adore you, everything about you!" He tried to gather her in his arms, but she turned away, nearly bumping right into Fari. "You are not a bargain. You are not!"

This statement clearly perplexed Fari, who was taking great pains to contain his growing erection.

Ki's words failed to have the desired effect on Elise, for she began to cry. "Leave me alone."

"Beloved." Ki reached for her again, but she hit him in the chest. This time hard, with both a punch and kick. It was enough to drive him out of the bed.

He landed on his back, air whistling from his lungs in a rush.

Fari scrambled up before Elise could round on him.

"Get out," she sobbed. "Both of you. *Get out.*"

Ki hesitated, as did Fari. Neither wished to leave Elise in her current state of upset.

She grabbed a pillow and launched it at Fari. It struck him hard in the chest, and fergilla hair burst from the seams and floated like fuzzy snow. Ki got to his feet and found his clothes, keeping his head low to ward off another such missile.

Fari joined him, staying a bit to his side and slightly behind as Ki put on his shirt.

Coward.

"Akad will be here shortly," Ki offered, sounding more hopeful than he felt. His tunic laces felt thick in his fingers, and he left them loose.

Elise threw another pillow at him as hard as she could, but missed. "Does he have a right to screw me too? Am I your whole ship's fuck-buddy now?"

"No!" It was Ki's turn to be horrified. He started back to Elise, to grab her and make her understand, but she tugged at a carved ivory spindle in the headboard. It popped free, giving her a fair weapon.

Fari grabbed Ki's arm. "Anon, brother. Leave her to the priest."

"But—" Ki tugged toward his *shanna,* who hissed and wielded the spindle like an OrTan pain stick.

"To the deck, Ki." This time, Fari's tone was amused, yet wary. "We can do no more here, for now."

Reluctantly, Ki followed his brother to the door. As the two men strode out of the portal, the ivory spindle struck the *pa*-covered wood beside Ki's right ear.

The clatter made him jump.

As he pulled the door closed, the last thing he heard was his precious *shanna* yelling, "And stay out!"

Ki and Fari stood and stared at the closed door. Behind them, the crew worked to keep the sails and riggings flawless, oiled, and properly turned on the largest ship in the Fleet. For that, the brothers were glad. Above them, the heavens offered thousands of twinkling stars, light to feed the *pa* and strengthen Ardani warriors. For that, the brothers were appreciative.

But in that cabin, behind that closed door, lay a sobbing creature they both had come to cherish. A woman they would give ship and life and even honor to nurture and protect. She hated them fiercely at the moment, seemingly because they both loved her. For that, the brothers felt strangely cursed.

"Do you think Akad understands enough about Earth culture to—" Fari began, but Ki cut him off with a wave.

His anguish at Elise's rejection and his anger over the circumstance mingled into one long growl of pain. "Females are females, no matter the culture. This is why I never wanted a soul's mate. Nothing but pain from here—that I can foresee, even without our sister Krysta's sharp and guarding eyes."

He started to stalk away, but Fari grabbed his arm. "Elise is alone, brother. Confused and hurt. She has been torn from her home, her family—"

"We are her family now!" Ki snatched his elbow from Fari's grasp.

On the decks behind them, men murmured and chuckled. Such was the first-mating time, when outworlder women were involved.

Ki, however, was not amused. He strode toward the main deck, intending to spend some time behind the hand-turned wheel. Exercise and a direct connection with his ship would do him good.

"Brother," Fari tried again, keeping pace. "We can ill afford this dissension. While you have been abed these last stellar days, we have taken three full OrTan assaults."

"What?" Ki stopped and whirled around. "Attacks? I thought those were regular battle dockings—slaver chasing. Why did you not fetch me?"

Your mind was elsewhere. Fari took the conversation private for the good of the crew, which Ki knew. The fact that his brother thought to do it first, however, only rankled him further. *In mating fervor, you would have been no use to me, even drugged.*

Do you so badly want the helm of this ship? Ki clenched his fists. *If I am no fit Sailmaster, then take it. When we dock on Arda, I will turn* Astoria *over to you and head into the hills. My madness would be better spent dashing rock against stone!*

You are overreacting. Fari's voice and expression were infuriatingly calm. *We all go mad when we first find our soul's mate. It settles with time, but—*

Ki cut him off by drawing his diamond blade. *There is no excuse for neglecting my ship. Either I am Sailmaster, or I am not.*

As you wish. Fari drew his blade as well. His was of sapphire, and made differently than Ki's, with barbs and spikes sprouting from every edge. What it lacked in strength, it made up for in treachery. One slice from that jagged blade, and an enemy would be rent and properly tortured.

Fari launched the first blow, catching Ki's blade full across. The sound was deafening, and even the *pa* in the sails flinched. In response, the ship lurched, throwing most deckhands to their backsides.

Grumbling broke out, then cheers as the brothers sparred. Ki's muscles roared, releasing his hurt and worry over Elise with each resounding clash.

Would she come to understand Ardani ways?

Would she forgive him all she had yet to learn?

Fari dodged in, then out—always quicker, but never stronger. It had always been this way when they exchanged jabs. Sometimes force won out, and sometimes speed. Usually, it was a contest of concentration. Ki intended to prove that Elise had not destroyed his focus.

He narrowed his eyes, slashing toward Fari with brute precision. Fari dodged, grabbing a rigging and swinging hard to the right.

"The OrTans are attacking because of your *shanna,*" he said. "They are intent on taking her back to Lord Gith."

With another powerful slash, Ki nearly caught Fari by the seat of his pants. "Then they are mad. Gith has no claim to her."

Fari swung again on the riggings, landing close to Ki and scoring a scratch on Ki's thigh. "They assert they do, that she was pleasured at Gith's will."

"He never touched her!" Ki lunged, ripping Fari's shirt open and off. He flicked it over the railings.

Breathless, Fari scrambled up netting, over Ki's head. *It was a* gasha *bed, brother. The OrTans have a record of it in their visual history.*

Ki blinked at his brother, then lowered his blade.

Fari let himself down from the riggings. "As you can see, we have a quandary."

The two brothers fell silent as Ki's mind turned over this new information.

Lord Gith did have a valid argument to the Council, then.

His fingers tightened on the hilt of his blade, and his teeth clenched. His *shanna* couldn't have known the significance of a *gasha* bed, nor could she have resisted it if she tried. But the fact remained that Gith's bed, at Gith's behest, would have brought Elise to climax. No creature could withstand pleasuring by a *gasha* without reaching orgasm.

And since she had found pleasure at Gith's command, however unwilling or unaware, OrTan law allowed Gith to claim her.

Or try to.

"I will never turn her over." Ki's voice was quiet, and it sounded mad even to him.

"I know, brother." Fari's tone was equally tense. He stood beside Ki, with the stars etching a pattern around his broad shoulders. "Nor would I. But you know where this likely leads."

Ki sighed.

Arda could withstand any number of OrTan assaults, of course. The OrTans were cunning, but they possessed little power or technology beyond the sexual pleasure chambers aboard skull ships.

Galactic peace, however, was a fragile thing. The Galactic Council had forged so many hearty treaties, allowing for the differences among planets, species, and values. Sex-slaving was illegal and frowned upon, but rules had been made for the practice's proper policing. Everyone knew the OrTans would never stop collecting populations for their pleasure, but at least they could be controlled, and no wars would erupt from the routine interception and defeat of skull ships.

When the time came for Ki to refuse Lord Gith's claim to Elise once again, when it was revealed that Ki had claimed, bonded, and bedded Elise as his soul's mate, Gith would fight him until death. If the OrTan high command so deigned it, there would be war. Any number of worlds might join on either side. All the damage, all the destruction—Ki had seen it before, when his father was Sailmaster, before the great peace.

War benefited no one.

Ki could not imagine losing the war, because Arda was too right and proud and powerful. Her allies would stand strong, but so many might die because of his folly. Because of his madness.

He shook his head. "I have traded sex for blood, brother."

"No!" Fari raised his barbed blade and slammed it into a plank between them. "You have claimed your true soul's mate, and ensured the survival of our line. You have done no more than any man would, no less than any Sailmaster should!"

Ki sheathed his diamond blade and looked at the stars. "I do love her."

Yes, I know.

I would die for her.

Fari's expression was serious. *As would I, but I hope it will not come to that.*

Until this conflict is settled, Elise will not be safe.

"Then we must protect her," Fari said quietly.

Ki leaned back against the ship's edge. He spread his arms along the soft *pa*-soaked wood. "Even if she wished to return to Earth, I could not allow it. She would be taken by the OrTans the moment we left her."

Fari's mouth fell open. "Return to Earth? But, the Law of Keeping—do you think she would ask that, even knowing what would happen to you?"

A fist of rage squeezed Ki's heart, then let it go. He took slow breaths, trying to fight the insanity of his mating fervor, even now rushing through his every vessel and pore. "I have not told her about the Law."

"You *have* gone mad." Fari pulled his blade from the plank and jammed it into his scabbard. "Tell her immediately, or I will!"

Ki lunged forward and caught his brother around the neck. Fari offered no resistance as Ki pulled him closer, until they were nose to nose. "You will not. I do not wish her to know. I have forbidden the priest to mention a word of it—long ago, before I even found my mate."

But, why, brother?

A movement behind them caught Ki's eye. It was Akad, heading for the cabin where Elise waited. She was probably crouching with a sharpened bed spindle or galley knife.

Ki's grip loosened, and he set Fari back on his feet. *I have not told Elise of the Law because if she stays, I wish her to stay out of love for me, truly and fully. Not out of some sense of guilt or obligation.*

For a moment, Fari said nothing. His expression was first tense, then worried, then sad. Finally, he showed only a slack-jawed acceptance. "It is a brave thing you do. And kinder than I thought you capable of being."

"It can be no other way, Fari. Elise must have true freedom to choose, and if she does not share the depth of my feelings—well, then." Ki dropped his gaze to the deck. "The Law will be my friend."

Chapter 5

Elise, now dressed in one of Ki's white tunics and ready for battle, lowered the spindle she had wrenched off the bed. The priest had been nice to her, but that didn't stop her from wanting to give him a rib-cracking kick when he quietly entered the cabin.

"What do you want?" she snarled.

Akad bowed his head once, then met her gaze. "I must begin your lessons, Grace. There is much for you to know before we dock on Arda."

"Like the fact that you're all perverts?"

"Per-verts?" The priest looked confused. His silver tattoos sparkled, and Elise could tell he was trying to work out the phrasing.

"Never mind." She sighed as she dropped the spindle on the bed and tightened the rope around her tunic. "Ki's a pig, and I want to go home. Will you help me escape?"

Akad's head snapped back as if she had slapped him. He opened his mouth, then closed it and went pale. "You are not a prisoner. If you desire to leave, the Sailmaster will arrange transport after we reach our home port."

"I don't believe you."

"Then you obviously fail to understand how much sway you have over your soul's mate." Akad slowly sat on the edge of the bed, keeping himself a reasonable distance from Elise's bed-spikes. "I understand your mistrust, but you have far more power than you understand. You hold the Sailmaster's heart, and his desire. He would do anything for you. If you do not wish to be mated with Ki Tul'Mar, he will help you return to Earth."

"Fine." Elise folded her arms. "The sooner the better."

The priest shifted in his purple robes, seeming uncomfortable and frightened all at once. "You should know, however, that the OrTans will claim you within stellar minutes of your return."

"What?" Elise sat straight up, and the priest flinched as the bed spindles clattered to the floor.

"Galactic politics are complicated, Grace." Akad glanced at his hands, then back to her. His dark eyes were wide and compelling, and Elise sensed nothing but honesty emanating from the Ardani holy man.

In quiet tones, Akad explained Lord Gith's suit to the Galactic Council, all the while keeping his gaze on his knuckles, especially as he discussed the part about the *gasha* being Lord Gith's private sex toy.

Elise sank back on her pillows, eyes closed. Her face was on fire. She felt so humiliated she didn't even care that there was an alien priest on her bed. "You're telling me they have all that on tape? Me, watching that sex show, and—and—"

"You did what was natural," Akad said earnestly. "No one can resist an OrTan sex machine. I assure you, every member of the Council knows that, and—"

"But they'll see me," Elise moaned. "All those strangers—a whole planet of alligators can watch me—oh, no. I thought I was alone."

"Is that what troubles you? That other people will see you unclothed and being pleasured?" Akad sounded shocked.

Elise opened her eyes, slack-jawed. "Of course that's what troubles me!"

For a moment, Akad only stared. Then he took a slow breath and released it with a heavy sigh. "Your forgiveness, Grace. Your untrained psi-strength made me forget how little you understand of our culture. For us, pleasure is as natural as—as breathing, or sleeping. The body and its charms and capacities, these are things to be celebrated, not hidden."

Elise briefly imagined Arda to be a beautiful Arthurian nudist colony, with giant orgies in progress around every corner, atop every hill and castle battlement.

"It isn't like that. I assure you." Akad actually smiled. "But we are a society of telepaths. Primitive concepts of modesty simply do not make sense for us."

Elise flushed an even hotter red. "I broadcast my thoughts about the orgies, didn't I?"

Akad nodded. "That is one of the reasons I am here, to teach you control and discretion. We find very few primitives with psi powers, but they must be trained. *You* must be trained, or you could harm others, or incite them to rage with your thoughts and impulses."

Elise sat up and tried to convince herself she was composed again. Her body literally ached from Ki's amorous handling, but she wasn't about to say that in front of a priest.

Then again, what Ardani priests did and didn't do—

"We are not forbidden to have sex like our Earth counterparts." Akad was smiling again. "Our society is far too old to believe in unnatural practices like celibacy."

Elise leaned forward to ask more about how Ardani priests lived, but something prickled at the back of her mind. What Akad had said earlier, about her concerns over the Council seeing her have an orgasm, kept replaying in her thoughts.

She frowned. "Akad, what *should* trouble me about Gith's stupid complaints?"

The priest sighed again, and his silver tattoos seemed to dim. "Grace, the OrTan's evidence is persuasive, and he *is* royalty. These things have great impact. I fear you should worry that Lord Gith will win his case."

"Oh." Air left Elise in a rush. "And what would happen then?"

"There would be war," the priest said matter-of-factly. "Ki will never surrender you. His family and his people—all Ardani—we will protect you."

Elise felt heavy, as if she had just swallowed concrete. "Y-Your people would go to war over me?"

"Without question." Akad's intense eyes burned a notch brighter. "Slavery is disgraceful and backward to us. We would never allow an Ardani citizen to be held against his or her will."

"But I'm not—"

"Yes, you are. When you joined with Ki, you became an Ardani citizen with full rights, privileges, and protections. Your fate is intertwined with ours evermore, Elise Tul'Mar."

"Elise Tul'Mar." Elise's heart rapped against her ribs. "Ardani citizen, wife of Ki, and...and...what? Sailmistress? Queen?"

"Queen is the closest equivalent." The priest nodded. His silver markings twinkled. "To be Sailmistress, you would have to win the honor in battle over the male warriors—which has happened, though not in recent millennia. Only he—or she—who can command all the Fleet's sails through force of will and mind may claim that title. And now, Grace, your lessons."

Elise stood. When she straightened her tunic, it swept around her knees but clung to every curve and dip. She felt self-conscious, but no matter how she tried to rearrange the garment, it stuck to her like glue. Or worse yet, a latex bodysuit.

For a moment, Akad didn't seem to notice her embarrassment. Then he stood, shook his head, and waved his hand.

Elise's tunic whipped over her head and landed on the bed, leaving her naked and dumbfounded in front of the priest. She tried to speak, but her words came out in coughs as her hands dropped to cover her breasts and the patch of hair easily visible to Akad.

"Do you think I have seen no women before you?" The priest's smile was patient, but his eyes were firm. "Lesson one. You are no longer on Earth. The shame and oppression of Earth's women are no longer yours to bear. Uncover yourself."

"But I—I don't really know you." Elise kept her hands in place. Her cheeks burned with the shame she was supposed to discard, just like that. She couldn't—and yet part of her wanted to believe this was all real, and no dream, and that it wouldn't end. To believe that she could be free with her body and pleasures, without having to face sermons and recriminations.

Akad folded his arms. "How well I know you—that matters not. I have no intention of offering you sexual attention, as you are not my mate, and neither you nor your husband has invited me into the marital bed."

"Now just a minute." Elise straightened, modesty be damned. "What the hell are you talking about? Mates, inviting you to the marital bed—what does that mean?"

The priest gestured to the table near the front of Ki's quarters.

Still acutely aware of her nakedness but resisting the urge to grab her tunic or a sheet, Elise followed him to the table and sat down in one of ten chairs. The wood felt smooth and cool against her ass, and her nipples brushed the table's edge. She shuddered, then gripped her chair arms and glared at Akad.

"When your body's sensitive spots are touched, you will respond." Once more, the priest sounded patient. "There is no shame in that."

"I don't want to talk about shame," Elise snapped. "I want to talk about other people in my bed."

Akad withdrew a silvery quill, a round inkwell, and a small piece of paper from his pockets. As he spoke, he lined them up in front of Elise. "On Arda, because we are telepaths, many relationships cross the boundaries you grew to accept as normal on Earth. The intimacy of thought-to-thought contact does away with false or useless modesties."

"Tell me about other people being welcome in my bed," Elise repeated. Sitting naked in front of the priest, feeling the chair against her bare behind—it was hard to think. She was getting wet, and that irritated her.

"Very well." Akad sat back in his chair. His eyes brushed her breasts, but his expression wasn't lewd or intrusive. Only appreciative, in a normal male way. "I will give you the abbreviated version, though I'm not certain you're prepared to understand or accept it."

Elise squirmed in the chair, her pussy getting wetter by the second. "Try me."

"Ardani mate for life." The priest met Elise's gaze. "They find a soul's mate. A *shanna*. Women call their soul's mate *sha*. Each couple establishes their own rules of marriage, of course, but traditionally, once couples are bound, they do not have sex outside the marriage unless their *sha* or *shanna* is present."

Akad paused, and Elise knew he was giving her time to react. "So, you're saying that Ki or I could fuck someone else, but only in—what, a threesome?"

"Three-some." The priest looked confused. "I do not know that word. You or your *sha* might choose to include others in your sex act. It is your choice and right as a couple."

"I see." Elise moved again. Her nipples were getting hard from the conversation, even though she wanted to be furious. "Do many couples do this?"

Akad shrugged. "All, that I'm aware of. The practice is common between brothers, sisters, and cousins—though never between parents and children, or other such generational crosses. It is natural to be attracted to the same-generation mates of your close relatives, as their tastes would be similar to your own. And it is natural for your mate's close relatives to find you attractive for the same reason."

Elise wished her body would cooperate with her outrage, but it ignored her. Her skin heated up, and she knew her clit had to be the size of a strawberry. Every time she moved, it ached. "So, I'm expected to find Ki's brother and sister attractive?"

"Not expected, no." Akad's expression reflected his difficulty understanding Elise's meaning. "It is just assumed, and permitted. Welcomed by most. Sex is about closeness and pleasure, and there is nothing wrong with being close to your chosen family."

Elise hooked her ankles together and squeezed her thighs to give herself some relief. Earlier in the morning, she had been wounded and enraged because Ki had wanted to share her. She still felt a little discomfort—but the thought that she had essentially married his knock-out of a brother, too, felt...exciting. Never mind the sister. She'd think about that later.

The priest folded his hands in his lap. "Do you have any questions?"

"You said the couple could invite 'others.' Does that mean anyone?"

"Yes." Akad's expression never changed, but his eyes traveled to Elise's breasts again. "Though physical intimacy is more typically kept between family members—yours, or your *sha*'s."

"I don't have any family except my cousin Georgia." Elise's excitement drained out of her as if she had pulled some inner plug. "And she's back on Earth."

Akad frowned. "That hurts you. I can see it, and feel it. A deep pain."

"Yes." Sudden tears spilled down Elise's cheeks. From horny to homesick in under five seconds. That had to be a record.

"Grace, one of the reasons I removed your clothing was to free you. To free your mind and heart so that your psychic abilities could manifest more fully." The priest leaned forward. "I encourage you to experience and resolve this grief, as it will hold you back from fully enjoying your *sha*."

"Or his brother and sister." Elise had nothing to wipe her tears, so she used the back of her hand. "Look, I won't just get over Georgia. You need to know that."

The priest was silent for a time, and then he sighed. "Then I encourage you to let go of the pain as much as you can. If your mind is open enough, you might be able to form some communication with Georgia, even though she's very far away."

That thought was too much for Elise, and she started crying harder.

Akad produced a handkerchief and comforted her with his presence until she regained control. Wanting some distraction, she pointed to the quill, inkwell, and paper in front of her. "What are these for?"

"To begin your psi training." Akad nodded toward the quill. "I plan to work with you today until you can lift the quill and dip it in ink. Without your hands."

"Okay, look. Out of everything you've said today, that's the craziest." Elise shook her head. "No way I can do that. Not a chance."

Akad's smile filled his whole face. "A disbeliever. Your excitement will be all the more great when you succeed."

* * * * *

"She asked for both of you." The priest spoke quietly to Ki and Fari.

Ki felt immediately wary. "Is she armed?"

"Only with more knowledge, Your Highness." Akad smiled. "I think she wishes to make amends, and to understand more about our ways."

"It is a trap." Fari clenched both fists. "If I enter that room with you, she will have a noose waiting beneath her pillow."

Akad shook his head. "You underestimate her. She is of great intelligence, and eager to learn and accept new things. As strong as Ardani females, and perhaps possessed of greater passion."

"And greater treachery," Fari murmured.

"How did she fare with the psi tasks?" Ki asked the priest as he patted his brother's shoulder to reassure him.

"Well." Akad smiled anew. "She managed a lift and placement of the quill. We were able to work on initial shielding strategies as well, so perhaps she will no longer broadcast her rage and passions to the crew."

"The men will be sorely disappointed." Ki laughed. "And she really wants to see us both?"

The priest nodded.

All the way to Ki's cabin, Fari discussed how to restrain Elise if she attacked by surprise. "I would not want her harmed," he emphasized, and seemed put out when Ki grinned.

"You are too serious, brother."

"And you are not serious enough," Fari retorted.

Ki went first into the cabin, and the first thing he noticed were lighted candles. His *shanna* must have mastered simple flames, or asked the priest to light them before he left. The yellow glow on the silver floors was relaxing, as was the light scent of bayflowers and brandywine.

Fari coughed, and Ki became aware of his brother's growing arousal. In a flash, he followed Fari's thoughts and gaze to the bed—where Elise reclined against the pillows. She was naked, and her hand was between her legs. Moving in slow circles.

"Akad told me I have power." Elise's voice was husky. "I want to see if he's right."

Her nipples seemed to swell under Ki's very gaze, and he felt all moisture leave his throat, headed south.

Fari groaned, and Ki knew his brother's excitement matched his own. Ki's *pa*-mark blazed in his skin, surging from his own feelings, multiplied by the emotions and thoughts of his *shanna* and his brother.

His cock throbbed, already at full length and strength.

Elise's hand kept moving. "Come here," she ordered. "Both of you. I don't know how much longer I can wait."

Intoxicated with the scent of woman-sex floating through the candle fragrance, Ki stripped out of his clothing. Fari did the same, revealing his own *pa* mark. It was wing-shaped, as if a great bird had branded his chest.

They approached the bed together, breathing almost as one.

Ki entered the bed on the left, and Fari on the right. Elise turned and kissed Ki deeply, still moving her hand between her legs. He caught her wrist gently and pulled it up.

"That is for us to do," he whispered.

Fari ran his lips across the back of Elise's wet fingers, drinking in her smell, tasting the sweetness he had been denied.

Ki saw that his brother's eyes were hooded. He was already lost in Elise, and no longer thinking of nooses.

Good.

Elise moved against Ki's body, pressing her breasts into his *pa*-mark and moaning as the silvery substance caressed her nipples.

Ki lifted her up and fastened his mouth on her breast. Her nipple swelling even more in his mouth rewarded him. "Yes." She groaned. "Please, yes."

He ran his tongue over the beaded flesh, and Fari's thoughts joined his own, following Elise's desires to the hot, wet slit between her legs.

As Ki pleasured his *shanna*'s nipples and mouth, Fari dipped into her quim, finding her clit with his eager tongue.

Thoughts and pleasure flowed between the brothers like water, with Elise's mind joining and retreating, joining and retreating.

"You wanted this," Ki rasped between kisses. "Stay with us. Feel it. Feel it!"

With a loud moan, Elise's mind touched theirs and stayed. She was almost totally joined with them, but maddeningly, it wasn't total. Ki knew this was likely because she was not Ardani, but he wished for the full bonding nonetheless—until Elise's demanding need drove away all other considerations.

She was very near climax. Fari gripped her hips and pulled her forward, drinking her, teasing and pressing, flicking his tongue through her slit in every way she imagined. Ki kept at her nipples and mouth, feeding her, pulling her to him and cradling her as she opened her legs wider and arched her hips.

In seconds, her body shook with release.

Ki felt her orgasm rattle through his own body. If he had not excellent self-control, he would have come when she did—but he held back. He wanted more. Much more.

In sync with Ki's intentions, Fari released Elise and sat back. Ki pressed Elise into the pillows, kissing her, settling himself between her legs. She moved against him, open and ready. Groaning, he slid into her quim. She rose to meet him.

Ki pumped, hearing himself growl as his pace grew faster. Harder. His *shanna's* arousal frenzied him, and Fari's desire for satisfaction drove him just as hard.

Once more, Ki slammed his cock into Elise. She shuddered and groaned, and both men felt the wash of her second orgasm.

Still, Ki held himself back, though he nearly chewed through his own lip doing so.

With quick deft motions, he pulled himself from Elise's wet quim, turned her over, and drew her to all-fours facing Fari. She gasped when she saw his brother's rod, but she didn't seem frightened. Only more aroused.

She was as lost in them as they were in her, and that simple knowledge nearly took Ki's control. Somehow, he kept himself in check, and entered her soft, moist slit again—this time from behind.

Elise groaned as he thrust into her, pulling her down against him. Her thoughts told Ki that her eyes were still on Fari, and that she wanted to touch him. She wanted to please him as they were being pleasured, and Ki quickly offered consent.

This was as it should be. More excitement, more fulfillment for those he loved.

His strokes intensified as Fari groaned. Ki could see Elise's mouth closing over his brother's swollen rod. Their connection allowed Ki to feel both at once—the joys of Elise's quim and the talents of her mouth and tongue.

His *shanna*'s thoughts were tied to his and to Fari's, and she felt both men approaching climax.

Do you understand your power now, beloved? Ki let his thoughts wrap around Elise like her wet slit wrapped around his driving cock.

Yes! As Elise rocked between them, giving herself fully to first one and then the other, she shouted her understanding. *Yes. Yes!*

Ki roared as he came, only a second before his brother.

Elise didn't pull away from either man. She milked them to empty, drained them like wells until both Ki and Fari had no choice but to leave the warmth of her body and collapse on the bed, panting.

As Ki drifted into an instant almost deadening sleep, he felt Elise running her fingers through his chest hair.

"I'm not bored yet," she whispered.

Chapter 6

Two stellar weeks later, Elise stood in front of Ki on *Astoria*'s sweeping bow. It was night, but Elise knew that only because she had glanced at the 26-section stellar clock before they left the Sailmaster's cabin. Each clock section represented a little less than an hour, and Elise had drawn a sun on the right and a moon on the left. The pictures helped her stay oriented. Unlike the odd mural of the wild women she kept meaning to ask Ki about. They didn't help her orientation at all, and in fact, they made her feel unsettled, somewhere deep inside.

Were there creatures like that on Arda?

Elise certainly hoped not.

Before she could bring up the wall painting, Ki began massaging her shoulders, rumpling her tunic as he gently squeezed her muscles with his strong hands. He kissed the top of her head, pressing his cock against her back, and she wondered lazily when he would discover she had left her underwear below deck.

The crew was about, but mostly amidship to stern. Elise had noticed that when she and Ki came on deck, the hands tended to give their Sailmaster and his woman a wide berth.

Excellent.

Tonight, she wanted Ki all to herself. Some stargazing, small talk, and then back to the cabin for more mind-altering sex.

The last two evenings, Fari had been with them, but the three nights before, they had chosen to be alone, like now. Elise found that she enjoyed herself either way, but sometimes, she wanted only her husband's touch. Ki seemed to feel the same way, though he left the decision of whether or not to include his brother completely up to Elise.

Fari was always warm and cordial to her, irrespective of invitations.

It's like having my cake, and eating it, too—whenever and however I want.

Elise smiled. She didn't know what to do about her sudden royal status, or about getting word of her whereabouts to Georgia—maybe getting Georgia to *Astoria* or Arda—but Elise did know one thing. She was never going back to Earth. Not to stay, anyway. The very thought of her life before Ki made her faintly ill.

At that moment, Ki's hands wandered over her breasts. Her nipples responded immediately, hardening against the silken fabric of her knee-length shirt. The tie around her waist was loose, and Ki pushed it open.

He stroked her midsection and kissed her ear, murmuring, "You are as beautiful as the stars, beloved. I hope our children will have hair like the sky's lights and eyes as blue as the Arda Sea."

"Mmm. I hope they're dark like you, with eyes like black pools and hair the color of space itself."

Ki chuckled. "Perhaps we should have many children, some fair and some dark."

"Do—um, do Ardani and humans from Earth have children the same way?" Elise leaned into Ki's chest as he caressed her breasts.

"Akad tells me yes, though Ardani gestation terms are shorter. With the combination of our slightly different biology, the priest thinks you will carry for around five months—a few weeks longer than a typical Ardani pregnancy."

"I'm assuming making a baby is similar." Elise sighed as Ki's hands moved lower, to her thighs, under the edges of her tunic.

"Yes, though I would need to know you are ready, that you desire conception." Ki's muscles tensed as he spoke.

Elise tried to track his thoughts, but he kept them quiet.

This must be important to him.

"If I say I want a baby, then tonight when we make love, you can just...see that it happens?"

Ki turned Elise around. His black eyes bored into her. "Please, do not tease me about something so beautiful. I know we have been together only a short time to your mind, but already I would catch the stars and make them your gifts. To fill you with my essence, to create life with you—it would be a sweet dream for me."

"Okay." Elise pressed her hands against Ki's rock-firm shoulders and kissed him. She took her time, tasting the faint salt of his lips, breathing his leathery musk. He let his hands travel up her legs until he cupped her ass—and discovered her bare skin.

Ki's rumble of male approval warmed Elise deep inside. With each kiss, each touch, he treated her like a goddess, like she was the only woman in the universe he truly desired.

I've only known him a few weeks. How can I want a child with him?

And yet she did. She wanted to feel him pounding into her pussy, and know that when he climaxed, he would give her a baby. The thought-to-thought connection dispensed with so much mistrust, so much fear, and so many misgivings. Elise knew what Ki was about. She knew what he thought, what he felt, and even some of his secret dreams.

All of them involved her.

Ki turned Elise back around to face the heavens and grazed her neck with his teeth. His caresses grew hungry, with one hand finding her nipples and the other moving straight for the wet slit between her legs.

"The crew," Elise whispered.

"They will keep to themselves." Ki bit her neck again, this time rolling her nipple between his thumb and forefinger.

Elise shuddered. His hands felt like fire on her chilled skin. *Astoria* shimmered in the dark of space, and Elise felt like she was riding a shooting star.

I want you, shanna. Here. Now.

Already, Ki was rubbing her swollen clit, and Elise could barely think. He could bring her to climax so quickly. Her breath came in ragged gasps as he moved her back against his cock, all the while keeping up his gentle, circular strokes on her aching clit.

Orgasm came like wind in the sails. Elise's whole body shook in Ki's embrace, and she heard herself cry out as Ki intensified his efforts, massaging her clit harder and harder to bring her to a second climax only seconds later.

He pressed his hand against her sensitive bud, letting the aftershocks roll through her as he nuzzled her neck.

His breath tickled and teased, and Elise wanted his lips on hers. Limp but ecstatic, she broke away, turned around, and kissed Ki. With shaking fingers, she unlaced his pants and let them fall to the deck. His pulsing cock pressed into her, and she gripped it with both hands.

Ki groaned.

Elise smiled, sliding her hands down his length. He was so warm and thick. She loved how it felt to rub from his tip and back to the heavy, soft sack behind. She loved the look of pained desire on his face when she did it, too.

Elise loved Ki. Every splendid inch of him.

"I want you inside me," she said. Her voice sounded like a hoarse whisper. "Fuck me. Now."

Obliging, Ki lifted her in one strong sweep, then lowered her onto his throbbing cock.

God, he felt good inside her.

She wrapped her legs around him and squeezed, letting him bury himself to the hilt.

So, so good. So completely filling and satisfying.

His strength was incredible as he moved her up and down, up and down, on his powerful length, grinding his hips against her each time she slapped against his thighs. Her breasts raked his chest, his face. A few times, he caught her nipple in his teeth. When he flicked his tongue against the sensitive flesh, jolts of pleasure made Elise cry out and dig her fingers into his neck.

Over Ki's shoulders, Elise could see the frigate's shining decks. And beyond that, the stars she used to see only through telescopes.

"Harder," she begged, and once more, Ki obliged. He rammed into her so forcefully her breath left in a rush. So hot and hard, like a molten flow within her.

She gripped him with her legs, pulling, urging him on. She was almost to the top, and she knew he would come when she did. She let her mind loose, pouring out her pleasure, her absolute enjoyment of Ki's every motion, scent, and sound.

The time was right.

The moment was perfect.

"I want a baby," she gasped. "I want your baby. Please. Do it. Do it now!"

Ki's eyes went wide as Elise climaxed. She rocked against him, once, twice, and then he exploded inside her.

Holding on with all her strength, Elise kept Ki's cock inside her. His breathing came in rough gasps, like her own gulps for air. He smelled of sweat and sex, and she adored him more.

"Did you?" she asked, surprised at her own soft, hopeful tone. "Will I be pregnant?"

After a rattling sigh of release, Ki smiled. "Yes, beloved."

* * * * *

Ki Tul'Mar knew he had lost control on the deck two nights before.

His *shanna* had wanted a baby, and he gave her one.

He had to be out of his mind.

Lord Gith's suit was no doubt before the Galactic Council. All of Arda might know about those troubles before they even knew their Sailmaster's mate. War was brewing. And Ki Tul'Mar had made a baby, a child to deliver into a mess that might not be settled any time soon.

I must be mad. I knew falling in love would rob me of my mind! Better that few know about the child, at least for a time.

Ki and Elise had already discussed this, and she seemed to understand and agree.

"Dock!" Ki shouted, and *Astoria*'s crew pulled her to a halt alongside the skull ship they had been tracking for four stellar days.

Ki held his position on the bow as crewmen looped the tethers. The hilt of his diamond blade rested against his palm.

When he was certain the ships were secured, he gave his next command. "Board!"

The rescue party bailed over the rail.

From the skull ship, OrTan slavers bellowed.

Swords flashed and clanked. Shouts filled the atmospheric containment.

Ki sprang off the bow, used the nearest sail to swing to the skull ship, and joined the fray. Three OrTans rushed him before his feet were firmly on the slaver ship's deck. He dodged to the right, and one of the beasts ran straight off the ship. The creature struck atmospheric barriers face-first, then slid from view.

Working dispassionately, Ki rid himself of the other two OrTans as if each were Gith. He felt like an automaton, a child's mechanical toy, as he labored.

Before Elise came to him, Ki had enjoyed the heat of combat, the challenge, the risk—but now it only frustrated him. He wanted to be with his *shanna*. He wanted to be the one protecting her instead of Fari.

But Fari was Sailkeeper, and security was his duty. *Astoria* was Ki's ship, his mission, his crew. He had to lead them.

Fari. Tell me she is safe.

There was a pause, and then, *She is safe. Focus on your purpose.*

His purpose. Yes.

In under two stellar weeks, *Astoria* would reach Arda, and Ki wanted this last victory fresh in the minds of his crew. He wanted tales of bravery and gallant rescues spread over Arda's mountains and forests. Most of all, he wanted Ardani pride running high, and trust in his leadership stronger than ever.

"To the hold!" He waved his sword over his head once.

Astoria's fighting men roared their approval.

In stellar minutes, the remaining OrTans had been knocked out, destroyed, or rendered helpless. Ki and his crew plowed into the slaving section, knocking open doors and sending rescues above-deck to have Akad remove their collars.

Once he secured the last of the captive's quarters, Ki waded through the groaning OrTans and grateful females to reach the priest for a head-count. Several Ardani speeders would be sent from the planetary dock to take the rescues back to their home planets. This was typically something *Astoria* would handle, but they were on course for home, due to dock planetside for Elise's introduction to her new planet.

Her subjects-to-be were eagerly planning bonfires and feasts in her honor. Krysta had seen to it that Camford's marbled halls and jeweled walls were polished with a woman's touch. Everything lay waiting.

"How many, Akad?" Ki drew even with the holy man and sheathed his sword.

"Moment," he wheezed. His voice was thin.

Ki glanced down and realized why.

A tiny Dini female was expressing her gratitude by demonstrating her oral talents on the priest. These women were no taller than a typical warrior's knees, but their ability to use tongue, lips, and teeth for a man's pleasure were legend across the settled universe.

The Dini sucked Akad's cock like her life depended on it. Her full, wet lips moved aside to show blunt lower incisors gently stroking the tender underside of his rod. Moving independently. They had minds of their own, those teeth. Ki knew that sensations—like ten fingers, two tongues, and several soft brushes working at once.

Akad's eyes were closed, and the woman's jaws worked hard and fast.

Hands tugged at Ki's breeches, and he realized there were three more Dini, ready to tend him. One slipped her thin hands into his waistband and gripped his mast, squeezing and releasing, squeezing and releasing.

Ki groaned as he thickened, but he pushed the small women away. "Thank you, no. I will take my pleasures with my *shanna*."

Ki. Elise's psi voice floated through his mind. *Are you aroused*?

He smiled, keeping hungry Dini mouths at a safe distance. *Ah. You noticed. Yes, I am, beloved. But only for you.*

Are you in battle?

The fighting is over. Why? Were you worried?

Yes. Elise sighed in his mind, and he felt a wave of chills travel his skin. *But now I'm just impatient. I'm touching my clit. Can you tell?*

By the Gods, he could. A feeling of soft wetness overtook his senses. Ki's cock went rock-hard in seconds, so hard it was almost painful. More sensations trickled through him, no doubt Elise's sweet excitement as she rubbed her clit—which he longed to flick his tongue against.

In front of him, the priest grunted as he came.

Ki ground his teeth. *Shanna, have mercy!*

She has no mercy. Fari's response was terse. *If you do not return, I will be forced to leave this cabin to relieve my own pressure, brother.*

In a rare flash of jealousy, Ki communicated his wish that Fari and Elise wait for him to begin any coupling.

Fari answered quickly. *Of course, brother. Though I cannot speak for what she will do to herself while I wait.*

Ki received his brother's mental image of Elise, naked across their bed. Her eyes were closed, and she was smiling. Clearly in the throes of passion. As Ki watched his brother's thoughts, Elise ran her fingers across her nipples and pinched them.

She did this over and over.

Ki's breathing quickened.

Shanna, I beg you! His plea was desperate.

Elise grinned and let her hand drop between her legs.

Ki shook his head to sever his psi flow from Fari. With one powerful stride, he reached the priest and grabbed

Akad's collar. "How many? How many rescues? Tell me now!"

Akad's wide eyes went wider. "Sixty-one, Your Highness."

"Will you see to getting them on the speeders?" Ki eased his grip on the priest's clothing.

"Of course, Sire."

Ki nodded.

He dropped the priest, hurried to the OrTan deck railing and hoisted himself to the rail. Using one of a dozen transfer planks now in place, he strode back to *Astoria,* down her silvery decks and steps, and into his cabin.

Fari was gone.

Elise was alone on their bed, still naked. Ki could feel the orgasm she had given herself, as if it hung in the air between them. He ached to be inside her, but battle grime clung to him like a putrid fog.

"Join me." He held out his hand.

Elise looked at him quizzically.

Ki bit back a groan as she shifted her splendid form on the bed, giving him a better view of her plump nipples and swollen quim.

"To the bath," he rasped.

And then Elise understood. She smiled, giving more warmth to the room. With the grace of a Chimera, she lifted her exquisite frame from the bed and came toward him.

He stripped off his clothing, and she followed him into their private bath chamber.

It took only a few stellar minutes to run the silvery bathing basin full of water that the *Astoria*'s engines generated as a byproduct. It was purified, of course, and as wholesome as the water rushing through Arda's many springs. Extra faucets added scents, herbs, and minerals, to soothe the mind and skin.

From flasks stored at bathside in a crystal cabinet, Elise selected a container of what she called "Jasmine," which to Ki was the subtle perfume of the lana-flower. She sprinkled it over the water's steaming surface, and sighed as the room filled with its fragrance.

Ki went first, lowering himself into the deep bath. Grime left him in a cloud, and the water bubbled and foamed as he rose.

Elise sat on the side of the basin with her legs just over the edge. Her look was one of love and interest, and great contentment.

"Do you feel better?" she asked.

Ki propelled himself to the basin's edge and hooked his arms behind Elise's knees. "In part."

She didn't resist as he slid her forward and ran his lips across her thighs. Her quim smelled of musk and sweetness, and she purred like a chitta when he kissed the blond triangle between her legs.

Wanting to take his time, Ki forced himself upward, to Elise's mouth, and kissed her. Her lips parted, drawing him closer. Her felt her dry flesh against his warm, damp chest, and his *pa* mark grew warmer than the bath.

"You are beautiful," he whispered.

Elise brushed his cheek with her palm, then let her fingers linger in the wet curls behind his ears. "You're too handsome for words."

"For me, there will never be another. Do you understand how important you are to me?"

His *shanna* smiled, then said simply, "Yes. You're the only man I've ever loved."

Their thoughts joined as fully as they could, and Ki kissed his soul's mate deeply. He tasted her neck afterward, and her shoulders. Water beaded on her breasts, and he licked the droplets.

She sighed.

Steam from the bath drifted through the chamber like lazy fog as Ki traced Elise's nipples with his lips, nibbling until she shuddered and thrust herself more fully into his mouth. His hands gripped her hips as he moved her to the very edge of the water, and then he sank to drink from her moist, intoxicating quim.

So swollen. His tongue brushed her clit gently, again and again, until she squirmed in his grasp. At that, he slipped two fingers into her slit, then three.

Elise moaned and arched forward. Ki drew his fingers out, then thrust them in deeper. Elise rocked against his hand, slowly at first, then faster and harder.

Beneath the water, Ki's cock was near to bursting as his beloved reached climax with a soft cry. Her body convulsed against his hand, treating him to more of her precious inner heat.

Gazing into her diamond-blue eyes, he lifted her from the edge of the bath, into the water, and into his embrace.

"I love you," she murmured, then groaned as he slid his mast far into her waiting quim.

Her eyes were still open, fixed on his as he lifted her up and down along his length.

Her fingers cupped his cheeks, and they moved slowly through the bath, as if engaged in the *Kon'pa* itself. The dance of life.

Ki concentrated on filling his *shanna*, as her thoughts directed him to do. Deeper. More powerfully.

"Yes," came her whisper. "Yes. More. I love you."

At the moment of peak, Ki knew if he hadn't given Elise a baby on the bow a few stellar stellar days ago, he would have done so at that moment. His feelings raged as deep as his cock, plumbing his *shanna's* depths, feeling glory in her total acceptance.

Her love drained him like an overfilled cup, and he sagged in her sweet embrace.

Life should be this sweet, always.

"Will I ever be able to join my whole mind with yours?" Elise's voice sounded dream-filled, yet disappointed.

Ki lifted his head. "In time, I hope so. Patience, beloved. With Akad's help—and as you grow accustomed to your new life, less will hold you back."

"Mmm." Elise pressed her face into Ki's neck, and seemed to be satisfied, but for one last sadness-filled thought.

Georgia.

Chapter 7

Elise focused on Akad's quill as it drifted in the air. It was a matter of perspective, she had discovered across the last stellar days, using the mind to move objects. Simply pushing the air back and bringing other matter forward.

All matter had *pa*, or life-force, as she had learned from the priest. That life-force, no matter how small, was like metal to the magnet of her mind. Of course, some types of matter had more *pa* than others. Items she considered inanimate on Earth—even those had *pa*, if only a trace.

Always knew that damned computer at work was alive.

In front of Elise, ink dripped from the quill's tip, but didn't fall to the cabin's silver floor or splash on her naked skin.

Concentrate. Focus....

The stray ink slowly returned to the tip of the quill.

"You are learning quickly." Akad's tone was full of admiration. "I would not have thought such progress possible. By the time we reach Arda, you will be ready for Presentation to our people. Impressive."

A smile played at Elise's lips. She rather liked being naked in front of Akad, because it did help her slay her inhibitions—but also because the sight of her aroused him. He would never say so, nor press her for anything improper, but giving an alien-priest a hard-on was still a thrill. Good thing she had learned to shield her thoughts most of the time.

This power thing is going to my head. Elise sighed. *If I don't concentrate, I'm going to make a serious mess.*

Using her thoughts, Elise moved the quill up and back, writing *Elise* in mid-air and holding the ink in place. In a fit of adolescent enjoyment, she added *loves Ki.* And then, *Ki loves Elise.*

Akad snickered. "Soon, you will be ready to handle pure *pa* as we do, to coat those things you desire to be more responsive to your thoughts. Amazing."

By day, she and Akad had been working on Ardani protocol and her psi skills. By night, Elise had been doing her best to wear Ki—and sometimes Fari—out.

Her pregnancy was still a private thing, with only Ki and Fari aware of it. Somehow, this increased Elise's enjoyment. Another secret treasure, like the sensations and feelings she had found with her new family of choice.

She should have felt wanton and ashamed, but all she felt was excited by the lingering images of her husband, her *sha,* pleasing her with the full force of his incredible cock. Fari didn't enter her pussy, but she had learned his strong, masculine taste as well as she had learned Ki's.

The more she worked with her mind, with the traces of *pa* in any object, the more she enjoyed sex. Just when she thought it couldn't get any better, it did. Elise could connect with Ki so fully—but not completely. It was frustrating. She wanted to give her full mind to her husband, but no matter how hard she tried, something always held her back. And she knew what it was.

Georgia.

Elise ached for the single loved one she had left behind on Earth.

It was a pain that wouldn't go away, but Ki's response to her requests to send word to Georgia—or better yet, go get her—had been met with refusals and attempts to explain and comfort.

It is forbidden. We cannot interfere with a primitive culture. What if someone finds the communication?

No, we cannot take a woman from Earth, even if she would come willingly. No interference. I am allowed you only because the OrTans had already taken you, beloved.

Even if it were not forbidden, the trip would be too dangerous. You are pregnant, shanna. War is brewing.

By the time we traveled there and back in a frigate, you would be half to delivery. We would need a speeder, and a speeder would be no match for an OrTan skull…

His reasons were endless, and all very rational. And yet, Georgia had to be out of her mind with worry, and grief, and loneliness. Elise wanted to relieve Georgia of those burdens, to give Georgia a chance at the new and exciting life Elise had discovered.

And Elise wanted her own grief to be resolved, so she could enjoy a deeper, more complete joining with Ki.

Her *sha* never complained, though. He seemed both pleased and surprised by how much thought and sensation they could share. When Elise touched the channels of *pa* marking her husband, she felt like she was touching his soul. And when he spoke to the sails, she felt the whisper of his voice all around her.

"I never want to leave this ship," she murmured, drawing hearts around Ki's name. The ink still wasn't dripping.

"Ah, these frigates are no place to live," Akad said. "Wait until you see the hills of Arda. And Camford. Such a castle—the Tul'Mars have ruled from Camford since the first recorded time on our planet."

"How long is that?" Elise lowered the quill and guided the ink back to its well. "In Earth years, I mean."

Akad watched as the last of the ink disappeared. "Stellar years are much the same as Earth years, but our lifespans are roughly ten times longer. Our recorded time began approximately 40,000 stellar years ago."

As Elise used her mind to twist the cap back on Akad's inkwell, she felt a surge of curiosity. "How old is Ki, then?"

"Our Sailmaster has lived one hundred and fifty stellar years."

"Oh." Elise grinned. *My old man. I'll have to tease him about that.*

"Fari is one hundred and twenty stellar years of age, in case you were wondering." The priest winked at her. "And with Ardani medicine, our healthy climate, and the strength of the Tul'Mar *pa* bonded with your own, you could very well outlive them both."

Elise returned Akad's training items to the table in the Sailmaster's quarters. She had learned a great many things in the last few weeks, sexual positions with one or two gorgeous warrior-hunks notwithstanding.

Her first impression of Arda as a gender and sexually liberated paradise hadn't been far from wrong. As Sailmaster, Ki was a king in the old-fashioned and total sense. He ruled Arda and all of her colonies, with assistance from his brother, sister, and cousins. Ardani citizens readily accepted the Tul'Mar rule, and Ki's family had a reputation for generosity beyond measure. No one on Arda went hungry or unclothed. They had no homeless shelters, few jails or courts, and virtually no crime.

All Ardani citizens were educated, and could continue their education at any time, free of charge—and judging from Akad's hints about the volumes of history and lore concerning Arda and the thousands of known inhabited planets, there would always be plenty to learn.

As the Sailmaster's wife, Elise would be viewed as a queen. She would be expected to become well-versed in the cultures, customs, and basic language of countless civilizations. This prospect both intimidated and excited her. She would be an equal in all affairs of state (as soon as she had a clue what they were), because by marrying Ki, she became not only an Ardani citizen, but also the only citizen *not* ruled by the will of the Sailmaster. Just as he was the only citizen not subject to *her* commands.

"It would unbalance the relationship," Akad had explained. "Even a Sailmaster needs someone who is his equal."

Bringing herself back to the present, Elise smiled. She certainly hoped *His Majesty* found her to be an equal. He seemed to. In fact, he seemed nearly perfect, as did the emotional and physical connection they shared.

Other than Georgia, the one worry Elise harbored was about that stupid mange-alligator Lord Gith, and his "claim" to her. Akad spoke little of it, and Ki refused to talk about it at all. Both men claimed that Gith's suit was inconsequential, because win or lose, Arda would never surrender their Sailmaster's mate.

Elise couldn't imagine a war over *her*, though. Most of the time, she pushed the thought aside, because she felt helpless to do anything about it.

"Okay," she said, holding out her hand to the priest, palm up. "You promised. If I could write my name with no spills, I could have some."

Akad's expression went from fascinated to worried in a matter of seconds. "Are you certain?"

"A deal's a deal, priest. Hand over the goods." When he hesitated, she added. "This is your queen talking. I can give you a direct command, right?"

Akad sighed. "Very well. Though I can't see what you need it for now." He reached into one of his pockets and took out a small brown vial. "You should be most accustomed to your husband's size and length, and—"

"And it's my business." Elise bent forward and kissed Akad's cheek. She made sure to let her breasts brush his robed chest, and she felt him shudder. "You're sure this drug poses no health risks—even if I were pregnant?"

"Correct, but I assure you, you could not be pregnant unless you and Ki planned for conception to occur. There are no accidental pregnancies on Arda."

Elise smiled. "If you'll excuse me, then, I have some things to do before my husband arrives. I only have a few minutes."

The priest bowed, gave one last glance to Elise's chest, and almost ran from the Sailmaster's quarters.

Elise gripped the vial he had given her as she used her thoughts to light candles.

Do I really want to do this?

She felt her anxiety rise, but battled it back. *It's a fantasy. But will I enjoy it in reality?*

The vial felt cool in her palm. She had prepared herself, trained her body as much as possible with what she had available. The liquid inside would assure that she at least felt little pain—and the payoff might be so worth it.

With some determination, she reached out to Ki's mind and made the invitation.

Bring Fari tonight.

It wasn't an invitation she made every evening, but it was one Ki had never refused. Tonight, Elise was counting on that.

She pulled off the vial's cap, drank the contents, then laid it on the table next to her training items. Her mouth tingled from the crème-de-menthe flavor of the Ardani relaxation potion, and she felt its effects almost immediately.

More than before, because I took more.

On unsteady legs, but with a surprisingly clear mind, she collected a small flask of natural oils and placed it on the bedside table, made her way to the bed, and arranged herself to greet her husband and his brother.

No sooner had she settled into the pillows than she heard the door open. Ki came striding in, followed by Fari. Both men looked flushed, as if they had hurried to answer her call.

Ah, power. Elise smiled. "That didn't take long."

Ki returned her smile with his own sexy grin. "Far be it for us to keep a lady waiting."

"What are you up to?" asked Fari.

"Always the suspicious one," Elise murmured. She heard her words slurring. "Why don't you both come find out? I promise you'll like it."

Elise wasn't sure who came out of his clothes faster, but Ki reached the bed first. He eased under the sheets beside her, and she ran her fingers over his firm muscles. Her lips found the tips of his dark hair, and she let it tickle her lips before she kissed him.

Some things—little gestures of affection, the rubbing of his *pa* mark, the feel of his cock inside her pussy—those were only for them to share. Other pleasures they both wished to give Fari, and his excitement and fulfillment pleasured them in return. Elise had grown so accustomed to the free sharing of desire and sex that she didn't feel embarrassed any more.

In fact, tonight, she wanted to take the sharing to another level.

If she could.

Her fingers found Ki's cock and worked from tip to sack. Semen beaded instantly, and Elise used it to oil her palm as she stroked him. Fari was kissing her shoulders. She could feel his hard rod pressed against her backside. Normally, after long and satisfying foreplay—and any number of orgasms—Elise would welcome Ki into her aching pussy while she took Fari into her mouth.

But not tonight.

You have taken the drug Akad gave you our first night. Ki's psi voice was surprised, but not upset. More intrigued.

Yes. Because I need to be relaxed.

But why, beloved? After all this time, have you come to fear us again?

"No," Elise said aloud. She ran her tongue over Ki's left nipple, letting her teeth tease the taut bud above one of his swirling *pa* marks. His muscles tensed, and she bit him gently again.

From behind her, Fari wrapped his arms around her and found her nipples. He pinched even as her teeth teased Ki. Bolts of pleasure shot through Elise, and she kissed her husband deeply.

Ki's cock pressed harder against her slippery slit, even as Fari's rod nudged her ass. She could feel Fari's throbbing rod, but he made no attempt to enter the wetness he was so close to. It wasn't forbidden by any law, but by custom and the rules Ki and Elise had established for their marriage. That part of Elise, that pleasure was for Ki alone, forever and always.

Elise had other surprises in store, however. Taking a deep breath, she allowed both men to see a mental image of what she had in mind.

For a moment, neither Ki nor Fari moved. Then Ki spoke. "Are you certain? It could be painful, especially this first time."

"That's why I took the drug." She kissed Ki again.

"I cannot," Fari murmured, half to her neck, half into her ear. "I do not wish to hurt you. The baby—"

"I've done my reading," Elise whispered. "No part of sex is problematic until my last two or three weeks. As for hurting me—use the oils on the nightstand, and just stop if I tell you to stop."

Ki gazed deep into her eyes, and she saw the depths of his ecstasy, worry, and wonder. He slipped his hand between her thighs, letting his fingers linger in the patch of soaked curls and move farther into her pussy.

Elise smiled at him, keeping his gaze as Fari smoothed the oil on his pulsing rod. When Fari returned to kneading her nipples, she felt the warm slick of the fluid across her pebbled peaks.

Ki dipped a single finger deep inside her pussy, then drew it upward until he was stroking her throbbing clit. Elise moaned and thrashed, but Fari reached down, ran his hand through her slit, added her moisture to his oiled rod, then lifted her leg up.

The drug didn't enhance sexual experiences, but it opened Elise to more of Ki's thoughts and feelings, more of Fari's barely controlled wanting. Ki kept his finger moving in and out, fucking her with his eyes and his hands. Elise could barely stand the pleasure of having her leg high, being so completely open to her husband's touch—but if he stopped, she'd die on the spot. His obsidian eyes seemed to swallow her whole as she climaxed, trying to squeeze her legs together, but feeling Fari keep them apart.

Ki slowed his strokes in her slit, but only long enough to allow Elise the briefest of respites. Then he started again, massaging her clit, rubbing it like a touchstone, working her higher and higher. Before she came again, he stopped, pulled her forward, and plunged his cock inside her pussy.

The sensation was incredible. Elise moved hard against him, and still Fari kept one of her legs high. She was wide open, and Ki's thrusts were gentle but deep.

And then she felt Fari, right where she had given him permission to be.

The tip of his moistened rod pressed against her buttocks, then into her ass, and slowly, ever so slowly, inside her from behind.

Ki slowed his motions as Fari moved higher and farther.

Elise groaned with pleasure and nerves, and then Fari was a little deeper, and a little deeper still.

There was pain, but then relief. The drug was working, and the oils made his entry smooth. She relaxed enough to let him in. Almost there. Almost completely filled—and then in one coordinated stroke, both men were inside her—Ki in her pussy, Fari occupying her ass. Elise groaned from the total ecstasy she felt. Any way she moved, pleasure exploded through her body. The line between agony and perfect pleasure blurred, and Elise's breath caught hard in her chest.

Her body tried to force Fari out, but he gently moved back in.

Ki matched his brother's stroke in her pussy, and Elise felt like the world's biggest cocks were fucking her everywhere.

And then the brothers began to move together, up and down, up and down. Her ass, her slit—both ached and felt satisfied in the same instant. She rocked between them, moaning, helpless against the intense bliss.

Her breasts pressed against Ki and she felt the heat of his *pa*. Like a living thing, it stroked her, touching her inside and out everywhere Ki's chest made contact. Behind her, Fari flexed and moaned as he pumped into her ass. His thrusts kept time with Ki's, in and out until Elise thought she might burst.

Ki's eyes were closed, and his face was a study in rapture as he moved.

His desire swirled through Elise's, lacing with Fari's excitement until Elise felt drunk, sober, and perfect all at once.

Every nerve in her body fired, and she screamed with the force of her orgasm. Her body shook and convulsed between the two men, ass and pussy contracting on both cocks, bringing them to climax almost instantly. Warmth filled her from the front and from behind, pushing her higher, and higher—and then she saw stars in a black night sky—and then she saw nothing at all.

* * * * *

Ki kept his head in his hands as Fari answered the priest. "She wanted us to."

"And if she wanted you to leap from the aft deck into the void, would you do that as well?" Fury crackled from the priest's very pores. "No, do not answer that. I suspect your response would be as foolish as your actions. She is not Ardani! To manage a psi connection of that force and power—both of you should be whipped."

Fari did not respond. Instead, he looked at his own hands and sighed.

Akad shook with the force of his convictions. "And she is pregnant. Your Highness. Pregnant, with all the perils ahead! Do you care nothing for her?"

Ki ground his teeth, and his stomach ached. No, it hurt. Like someone clawed at his guts. Elise's scent yet lingered on his fingers, even as she lay unconscious in the priest's port chamber. "How long before she wakes? How long before I may speak to her?"

"Who can say?" Akad treated him to a withering frown. "I have contacted Krysta, and she is bringing her speeder to meet us. May the Gods pray she has better sense than the both of you."

"We did not know she would be harmed!" Fari grabbed the priest's shoulder. "We would never consent to anything dangerous for Elise. Her psi talents—we thought she was capable. Safe to couple with the both of us."

Akad shook his head. "An excellent speech. Perhaps you will give it to the people who have assembled for her Presentation? She will no doubt sleep through that, at least."

Ki stood and strode away from the conflict, into the chamber where Elise lay in her stupor. The argument behind him only increased his frustration, and his heart ached as he beheld his still, pale soul's mate. Keeping a piece of his mind on the sails, urging his ship toward Arda at top speed, he bent over and kissed her warm brow.

Hear me, beloved. I am eternally sorry. Had I but known…

Akad said the strength of their combined physical and mental connections overwhelmed Elise's lesser psi skills. To be connected with two sources of enhanced *pa,* it was too much for her synapses, and her brain simply turned off her consciousness to protect her life.

If she failed to wake, Ki would fling himself into airless space.

He had known her only a few score of stellar days, but she was everything to him. His heart's partner. His soul's mate. Every moment, she surprised him anew, and drew him closer to her. He did not know if he could survive without her.

These things he whispered in her ear.

Then, settling beside the bed, Ki took Elise's hand and ran his lips over her fingers. For a time, he whispered poetry to his *shanna,* then hummed songs known on his planet for thousands of stellar years. Healing songs. Songs of regret, and of love.

In a while, Fari joined him. Akad had huffed away to the bow to await Krysta's speeder.

"Has she stirred?" Fari asked.

Ki shook his head. "Her thoughts are quiet."

"I am so sorry, brother. This is my fault."

Fari's anguish coated his words, and Ki cut him a sharp frown. "This was no more your doing than mine. We have both been besotted. Surprised and intrigued. From here, we learn from mistakes and exercise more caution."

"I will make this up to you. To her."

"You owe me nothing." Ki kissed Elise's hand. "Except to find your own *shanna,* and expand our family. Grow our love. Elise deserves nothing less than all the joy we might give her."

With a sigh, Fari fell silent. He took up a post at the foot of Elise's bed, and there he remained until late in the afternoon, when the brothers heard *Astoria*'s docking horn.

"I will go to greet Krysta," Fari offered.

Ki nodded. He found he did not want to let go of Elise's hand, and he did not want her to go to Arda without him. That was foolish, of course. She would receive much better medical attention at Camford, and there would be no risks from battle.

Stellar minutes passed as Ki studied his sleeping bride, and he found he had run out of words. As he slipped from his chair and knelt at her bedside, thoughts were all that remained, and prayers, and hopes.

You are so strong, beloved. Please, return to me. Let me show my sorrow in a thousand reparations.

"Well, well," said a rich female voice from behind him. "It is about time a woman humbled you."

Through his fog of fear and concern, Ki felt a shimmer of relief. "Krysta."

He stood and turned, greeting his younger sister with a fierce embrace. She was as tall as Fari and almost as strong, and her hair and eyes were as dark and mysterious as starless space. Still, Krysta radiated an undeniable light, and her presence steadied and comforted Ki.

"Take heart, brother." Krysta pushed back from him and gazed at Elise. "Akad says your feral mate has strength beyond our understanding."

"From his lips to the stars." Ki let out a rattling breath. "I curse myself for this misjudgment."

Krysta continued to study Elise, taking in the lighter-haired woman's lanky yet petite frame. "Is it true that she is with child?"

Ki felt his cheeks color. "Yes."

To his surprise, Krysta grinned. "Good. Cheers to both of you! To the dreg pools with Lord Gith and his foolish pursuits."

A smile tugged at Ki's mouth. "Thank you, sister."

Krysta met his eyes, then hugged him again. "I need to bear her home now. Can you let her go?"

"I—I—" Ki's words failed him. He had never felt so clumsy and useless in all of his stellar years. "Yes. I will carry her."

"Let me take her." Krysta squeezed his shoulders. "Wait until you hear the departure horn. It will be easier than watching me spirit her away."

Ki struggled with his urge to fight Krysta's wisdom, but in many things, women knew best. That much he had learned from his powerful, intelligent mother, before she was killed with his father in an OrTan raid on his father's vacationing speeder.

"As you wish," he muttered.

"I will care for her like my own firstborn." Krysta's tone was reassuring. "In a stellar week, she will be hale again. Trust me."

"Without question or doubt." Ki knew his positive words were forced, but he did believe in his sister's caretaking and healing abilities. "May the stars speed you home."

Krysta stooped and swept Elise into her arms as if Elise were indeed a child.

Before Ki could object or change his mind, she turned and carried her new sister-in-law away from the chamber.

Chapter 8

Elise woke to real sunshine and naturally fresh air. For a brief moment, she thought she was on Earth, in her apartment—but her brain told her that wasn't true. Her next thought was that she was still in space, on Ki's frigate, but no. Not there either. The light hum and the sense of motion she had known for a few days longer than an Earth month—gone.

She was in a large bed, almost twice the size of the largest mattress she had ever seen. The bed was high off the floor, and curtained like the one in Ki's quarters on the *Astoria*. Gauzy drapes were pulled aside and tied to reveal a room the size of a small cathedral—warmer, but no less ornate. The walls were made of sculpted gray stone, with what looked like carved ivory inlays. Silken tapestries covered many sections, splashes of yellows, blues, greens, and reds on the smooth rock. A large stone fireplace dominated the wall opposite Elise's bed.

On the room's long right wall, the ever-present three wild women gazed at Elise from couches made of flowers and vines. Always naked, always fangs bared. Did they have to be everywhere?

She sat slowly, feeling dizzy and confused.

This had to be Arda. Camford—Ki's castle. But how did she get here? What happened?

The last thing she remembered was being with Ki and Fari, having perhaps the best orgasm she had ever experienced, feeling so close to them, and—oh.

"Oh, no!" Elise rested a hand on her stomach.

The baby! Was the baby still—?

A feeling of well-being came over her as she rubbed her belly through a sheer, cotton-like gown. Her baby was alive, still inside her. Thriving. She didn't know how she knew that, but she did. Something whispered in her mind and heart, and she knew that whisper came from her unborn child.

Good heavens. Will I be able to hear this baby speaking and crying before she's born?

She? Is the baby definitely a she?

Questions for Ki, as soon as she saw him.

For a moment, Elise simply smiled. She felt exquisitely female, and safe and happy. But where was Ki, anyway? Weren't handsome heroes supposed to be kneeling at your bedside after you woke from being ill, or unconscious, or nearly fucked to death?

Then again, the room was so huge, he might be in some corner she couldn't see, or in a bath chamber, or taking a leak.

"Ki?"

Her voice sounded small in the huge room.

Elise shivered, pushing away the memory of the last time she woke alone in a bed. Made of air. On an alien slave ship.

Dear God. Gith. What if that alligator bastard—

A scraping sound made her jump.

The heavy wooden door to the room burst open, and a woman strode over the threshold. She was tall and thin, yet muscled, and clad in form-fitting black leather. At least it looked like leather. Her long hair and large eyes were so dark they seemed to shine with blue highlights, and silvery designs covered her chest and neck. The soft *pa* pattern on her skin reminded Elise of cherry blossoms.

As the door settled behind the stranger, Elise's first impression was that Fari had undergone a sex change, and that the surgeon had done an excellent job making him stunningly perfect.

And then it struck her. "Are you Krysta? Ki's sister?"

The woman flashed a bright smile. "Indeed. Welcome home, mate of my brother, though I would have preferred you arriving awake and not so ill used."

"I—I wasn't ill used, really." Elise pulled up her sheet because she had the feeling Krysta was staring at her breasts. Which was only fair, given that Elise was having a hard time keeping her eyes off her sister-in-law's silver-patterned cleavage. "Guess we got carried away."

Krysta nodded. "Akad said the psi energy of such a full coupling was too much for you. But now we know, and we will be more careful."

We? Elise's heart beat a little faster. Krysta said *we*, not *they*. As if she expected to be a part of future…um, full couplings.

Okay, so Elise had been having sex with not one but two warrior gods.

But Krysta was a woman.

Elise had never thought about having sex with a woman. Never found a woman attractive in that way—but wait. That was a lie, wasn't it?

Georgia. She's so beautiful.

Georgia was family, but in truth a distant relation at best. There was nothing wrong with appreciating her beauty. With wanting to hold her, and enjoy her.

Without warning, sadness overwhelmed Elise, and she started to cry.

Krysta rushed to the bed and climbed in beside Elise, like a teen at a slumber party. She took Elise's hands in her own larger ones and held them tightly. "What upset you, sister? Was it something I said? Should I fetch Ki? He is outside, on the archery range with Fari."

Elise shook her head, but found she couldn't speak. The lump in her throat felt too big to swallow.

"Ki is not beside you because I chased him out—Fari, too. They needed fresh air, and to gather their senses." Krysta sighed. "My timing was poor. Apologies, Elise."

"It's not that." Elise pulled one hand free and patted Krysta's shoulder. In spite of her nervousness, she felt instantly comfortable with the woman, who was so clearly kin to the man she loved. "Seeing you, I just—I thought about someone I left behind on Earth. My cousin, but we were raised like sisters."

Krysta's expression shifted from distress to relief to sad understanding. "Ki made mention of this. Her name is Georgia?"

"Yes." Tears spilled down Elise's cheeks again. "I've asked him to send a message, or take me back to get her, but he refuses."

"It is too dangerous! The baby, the OrTans—"

Elise pulled away from Krysta. "Yes, I know. I've heard it all from Ki. But Georgia thinks I'm kidnapped or dead. She's probably grieving herself sick."

Once more, Krysta's beautiful, angled face reflected sadness. "This must be very difficult for you, losing your home, being stripped of all that is familiar to you."

"Not really." Elise sank back against her pillows, leaving Krysta sitting above her. She didn't protest when Krysta took her hand again, even when Krysta lifted it to her feather-soft lips and kissed it gently. "My life before Ki was stifled. Useless and boring. I don't want to go back to Earth at all, except to get Georgia. She'd come with me. I just know it."

Krysta said nothing, and Elise knew there was nothing to say.

Forbidden. Too dangerous. A thousand reasons, and I don't give a damn. Elise sniffed. *Unless I figure out how to get to Earth myself, I'll never see Georgia again.*

To distract her new sister from her sorrows, Krysta told Elise about flying to meet *Astoria*.

"I nearly had to fight Ki to retrieve you," she said. Her rich voice sent shivers through Elise, who still couldn't get used to the fact that her husband's family wasn't sexually off limits. That she was married, but free to think, to fantasize—even about such Earth-forbidden things as Ki's sister.

"By the time Ki docked planetside," Krysta continued, "he was beside himself. He missed you so deeply. One stellar week away from you, and my oh-so-arrogant brother was nearly ruined."

Krysta explained that the kingdom of Arda had been informed that Ki Tul'Mar's mate was ill, and bonfires dotted every hillside. There were dances and songs. Old medicine, to speed the healing efforts of Krysta and the priests.

Krysta said Ki had barely left the bedchamber, and Fari spent hours a day checking to see if Elise had stirred.

"They have been pathetic, really. Men are so strong, and yet so child-like at times. Led around by their cocks—it is too easy." Krysta smiled.

Elise reminded herself that this seemingly young woman was nearly four times her age, and she wondered how many lovers Krysta had known.

Enough to put me to shame, no doubt.

"Krysta, what happens from here? I mean, what happens next, for me?"

Ki's sister bent down and kissed Elise on the lips. Krysta smelled of mint and spring flowers, and her leather-clad breasts felt soft against Elise's thinly veiled nipples.

"You are beautiful," Krysta murmured. "And your mind is so bright. Ki described you well." She trailed one hand up and down Elise's arm. Such a soft touch, almost a tickle, exciting and maddening at the same time.

Elise's mind swam as Krysta reached for her thoughts. Elise didn't resist the mind-intimacy. She wanted to know Krysta—but she felt nervous. Self-conscious. And she felt her nipples tightening. The dampness in her pussy was immediate, and surprising. She fought an urge to pull away, and an equally strong urge to melt into the next kiss, to see what a woman's mouth really tasted like.

Krysta seemed to sense her ambivalence. She moved back, kissed Elise's forehead, and smiled. "What happens next is that you rest and recover. Find your land legs, see your new home—and then we will reschedule your Presentation. Once the Law is satisfied, you will have much time to continue your training. And learning, and exploring."

"You make it sound simple."

Krysta crawled off the bed, laughing. "It will be, sister. Have faith. You are welcome here, and everyone will see to your comforts."

"Where are you going?" Elise gripped her sheet again, suddenly wishing Krysta's warm, graceful body were back beside her. She felt cold, and too alone as Ki's sister headed for the chamber door.

"Patience, please. I am off to fetch my brother, lest he take me to task for not hailing him the moment you woke."

The moment Krysta departed, Elise climbed out of the huge bed and located the bathroom at the back of the chamber. It was much larger than *Astoria*'s simple bench and face basin—in fact, it was about as large as the Sailmaster's quarters—though the toilet was still a bench. With several seats.

Jeez. Do these people share everything?

The bath basin seemed gigantic—a combination small swimming pool and whirlpool—with multiple faucets against the far wall. The sink basin was also huge, big enough for five or six people to share, and backed by a swirling ivory frame with an inlaid mirror.

Elise took stock of herself, and felt mildly surprised by what she saw. Her skin had a slight pallor, but otherwise, she looked healthier than ever. Her hair had been recently combed. It had a rich golden sheen, and her muscles felt supple and strong.

Ardani medicine must be as good as Akad claimed.

Moving her hands slowly over her soft gown, Elise touched her still-beaded nipples. Gentle thrills traveled up and down her spine, and she took a deep breath. The bathroom was beautiful. She felt beautiful. Everything about Arda seemed sensual and alluring.

So far.

Was it possible to have sex several times a day, every day, for hundreds of years?

She just might find out.

Elise used the facilities quickly, cleaned herself with sweet-smelling water and soft cloths, and ran what looked like a pearl-handled comb through her hair. For a second, she considered removing the sheer gown, but decided to leave it. The downy fabric felt good against her skin.

"Beloved!" Ki's voice rang through the chamber, followed by the hollow thump of a wooden door.

Elise ran out of the bath chamber, across the marbled floor, and straight into Ki's waiting embrace.

"My *shanna,*" he murmured, kissing her hair, her face, her neck, holding her so tightly she could barely draw a breath. "I was so worried. How I missed you!"

"I love you." Elise fell into his kiss, already breathless because his hands seemed to be everywhere at once. He caressed her, rubbing the gown's satin fabric against her hips, her backside, her breasts.

She ached for his teeth on her nipples, the firm weight of his muscled body, the feel of his thick cock, pumping inside her slit.

Ki swept her off her feet, carried her to the bed, and stretched her out beneath him. He was out of his clothes in seconds, all the while keeping his blacker-than-black eyes locked on hers.

His cock was enormous. Elise felt the hot hardness against her thighs as he stretched over her and lowered himself for a long, deep kiss.

Their thoughts joined as much as they could, and Elise felt Ki's pleasure as he slid the flimsy gown up, over her breasts, and let it pool on her chest. He tried to restrain himself, but his excitement had an almost desperate edge as he fastened his mouth on her breast.

Elise moaned as he flicked her nipple with his warm tongue. He squeezed the other nipple roughly, but not too rough.

When she thought she couldn't stand another second, Ki switched, treating the other breast to his mouth and working her wet, swollen nipple with his fingers.

"I want you inside my pussy," Elise demanded, spreading her legs.

Ki's heated gaze bored into her, and she felt the urgency of his need. She gloried in it.

He settled himself on his knees, holding her thighs apart. His magnificent cock stood straight out, tantalizingly close to where Elise wanted him to be.

With one finger, he traced the triangle around her sex, moving toward her slit with maddening slowness.

Elise groaned and pushed her hips off the bed—and his finger found her pulsing clit. Like a laser. Like a magnet. The exact spot. In just a few strokes, she came with a sharp cry. And then Ki's fingers plunged deep inside her, pussy and ass.

Like before, but all Ki.

The fullness, the ecstasy—no relaxing drug, and no pain.

Elise gasped and bucked, lost in pleasure. Lost in the feel of his hands in her most intimate areas. Absorbed by his joy at her warmth and wetness.

Slowly at first, then harder and faster, he pushed into her. She rocked and bounced against his hand, savoring the dual sensation until she came again, squeezing her legs against his arms.

"I love you with all my heart," he said in a low, rasping voice. His teeth were clenched as he slid his fingers from her drenched, throbbing slit, and Elise knew how much he needed relief.

Once more, she spread her legs as wide as she could. "Don't make me wait any more. And don't hold back. I'm well. I swear."

Ki growled and hoisted himself over her. In one hard stroke, he buried himself deep. Elise moaned and rose to meet him as he drove into her again, and again.

"Fuck me," she begged. "All of your cock. Harder!"

The noises roiling from Ki's throat sounded wild. Almost bestial. He slammed into Elise so hard her body rocked back against the pillows. The whole bed seemed to move.

Their bodies pressed together in sweat-sheened perfection.

Another forceful plunge, and Ki came with a guttural shout. Elise felt his warm fluids filling her to the brim, and then incredibly he kept going. Pressing still harder and higher. Elise felt herself climbing the ladder again, and in seconds, her body shook with orgasm as Ki once more spilled himself in her slit.

Before she could react, he pulled out, and Elise was shocked to realize he was already growing hard again.

"Can you continue?" Ki whispered. His expression was dazed. Enraptured. "I do not wish to take your strength."

"I'm fine." Elise heard the tremor in her voice. "Take what you want, however you want it."

Moaning, Ki pulled her forward, spread her legs as wide as possible, then helped her put her legs on his shoulders.

Her heart hammered.

What was he doing?

"Relax," he murmured, pressing his cock against her ass. "Let me in."

Elise groaned from the mere thought. She reached up and rubbed her clit, keeping herself primed. "I want you."

There was a flash of pain—and then his cock filled her ass. So big, so total. Elise felt impaled, but not painfully so. Perfectly so.

"So tight," he gasped, knowing from her thoughts that he wasn't hurting her.

Elise let out a throaty groan, relishing the full, erotic sensation.

Ki rocked against her, taking it slow and easy, then building. And building.

"Yes." Elise felt herself close to another orgasm. This man was unbelievable. Everything he did drove her to new heights.

"Come," Ki commanded, pounding into her ass. He drew his thumb across her clit, and that was all it took.

She shrieked as her muscles tightened around him. He joined her then, at last emptying himself completely as she twisted and jammed herself against his sack and thighs.

For a moment, they didn't move.

They couldn't move.

Elise felt the pressure of his cock still inside her, and the weight of his hand pressing against her mons, easing her down toward slumber.

And then Ki slipped himself free.

"You are splendid, and I love you with my very soul." He bent and kissed her, and she tasted the salt of his sweet exhaustion.

"*Sha*." She touched his face. "Beloved. Forever my beloved."

* * * * *

Ki Tul'Mar did not leave his private chambers for three stellar days. His *shanna* pleasured him over and over, satiating the terrible need that had consumed him while she lay ill.

Her heart and generosity knew no bounds.

And he had never been so afraid of losing anything or anyone in his life.

Each time he looked at Elise, each time he felt the softness of her flesh beneath his hands—he thanked the universe for her presence, and her recovery.

Now, a stellar week after her waking, she had resumed her lessons with Akad, the occasional inclusion of Fari in their marital pleasures, and the seeking of new experiences. In fact, she had been exploring Arda with a fervor.

"The mountains are so tall and green," she had told him over dinner last evening. "The grass looks like a pelt on the slopes."

And, "Ki, the water here is so beautiful and sweet! It tastes fresh and cool, no matter where I drink it."

And, "I had no idea Camford was as big as a city. It's incredible!"

Her ecstasy at the herds of supple Chimera flowing over the grounds knew no bounds as well. "They look like giraffe-horses! And so many colors—they keep changing. Look! There's a purple one."

This particular morning, after *Kon'pa* and a leisurely coupling, Elise had dressed in loose breeches and a white tunic. Leaving Ki to breakfast in the great hall alone, she headed out early for a riding lesson with Krysta. After that, Krysta intended to teach Elise the basics of flying a speeder.

"She will be a natural pilot, brother. I know it." Krysta's excitement at finding another female with an adventuresome spirit had been apparent.

Most women on Arda could ride and pilot, at least at a rudimentary level, but many preferred to leave those duties to men. Ardani females were robust hikers, mountain climbers, and runners, and they preferred the taming of game birds, water sports, and carving for pastimes. There was no prohibition against women training as warriors and joining the Fleet, but few chose to do it.

Krysta, of course, was an exception. She was captain of the Home Guard, and she spearheaded a group of lightly-armed speeders that would be Arda's first line of defense against direct invasion.

Knowing Ki's luck, Elise would wish to join this vanguard, and worry him into an early grave.

"Beautiful morning, brother." Fari entered from the great hall's main door. He strode past the many planetary banners adorning the walls, pulled out a chair beside Ki, and helped himself to all of the five serving dishes of eggs, chaka-meat, hashed tubers, steaming bread, and fresh gravy.

"Did you see Elise and Krysta out in the yard?" Ki took a swig of golden sweetberry juice.

"Yes. Early, on my morning run, they nearly trampled me. That Chimera of Krysta's—no discipline. And now she is teaching your wife all of her bad training habits."

Ki grinned. "Krysta does spoil the animals."

"Just now, when I crossed the outer bailey, Krysta's speeder swooped low and nearly shaved the top of my head. If I am not mistaken, your lovely *shanna* had the controls."

"She learns quickly." Ki sat back, feeling full and pleased. "You need your own soul's mate soon, brother. There is nothing better."

Fari shook his head. "Thank you, no. I prefer enjoying yours now and again. Better for the mind. At least I can think of things other than her wet quim. Unlike you."

At this, Ki's cock hardened. He laughed, but then the warning in his brother's tone penetrated his Elise-besotted brain. "You bring news of Gith's suit?"

"Of many things. But firstly, the OrTan's claim." Fari's expression tightened. "The Galactic Council refused to dismiss it out of hand. They will hear the case."

Ki's gut clenched. Unpleasant news. The Council must be predisposed to favor Lord Gith's assertions, or they would have quashed the case to avoid angering Arda.

Fari's grim frown confirmed those suspicions. "I think it essential that we present Elise to the people before the suit moves forward, Ki. Let them see her beauty and light, and know the depth of your love for her. It will only solidify popular support."

"Wise words." Ki leaned forward and rested his arms on the table. "Akad believes she will be ready to handle pure *pa* in two stellar weeks. Three at the latest."

"That gives us little time." Fari grimaced. But he knew, as Ki did, that handling *pa* was a necessary part of the Presentation.

Elise would be required to stand before her subjects and allow their limited touch to her thoughts. The people would weigh her goodness, sincerity, and worth. They would verify the truth of Ki's love for his chosen bride.

Then, to demonstrate her solidarity with Arda, Elise would coat her hands in *pa* and make her mark on the Wall of Life, outside the gates of Camford.

After that, Akad, as Arda's high priest, would formally ask Elise for her pledge to Ki. She would have to agree that no matter what the circumstances, she would never abandon her mate.

If she affirmed the pledge, the Law of Keeping would be satisfied.

If she refused to make the pledge, Ki would lose his status as Sailmaster—and his life. Ki's honor and virility would be forever soiled, and his time would come to an unpleasant end. A beheading on the ancient and little-used Tuscan Platform, deep in the Camford Forest.

And he would deserve it.

A ruler who could not win his own soul's mate was, in the eyes of Ardani history, no man, and no fit ruler at all.

"You still have not told her, have you?" Fari's question sounded gentle. A concern, not a condemnation.

"No." Ki's firm tone surprised even him. "And she will not be told."

"It—it should not be an issue. She will affirm, brother. Her heart, her very being, belongs to you and you alone. It is obvious in her every gaze, her every touch."

"I believe it so, yes." Ki managed a smile. "But it will be an anxious moment, to have my existence ride upon a single spoken word."

"You have won your mate, brother. Take comfort, and be joyful." Fari finished his meal and sat back. "And now, we have much to consider. Our defenses need work before open warfare with the OrTans."

"Indeed." Ki motioned for one of the many servants, all employed by Camford at their own choice and well-paid for their labor.

As two buxom women hurried forward to clear the table, Arda's ruler stood with his brother and strode from the great hall, heading south and down, deep within the castle's bowels. To Camford's most secure area.

To the war room.

Chapter 9

Elise guided Krysta's shining speeder over Camford Lake, admiring its emerald waves. Her soft white tunic wrapped her body like a comforting hug, and her loose breeches hung gently against her legs. The speeder's burnished floor felt cool but comfortable on her bare feet.

She felt free. Completely unfettered. And she loved flying. Every morning, after dancing the *Kon'pa* with her husband (typically followed by slow, toe-tingling sex), Ki, Fari, and Krysta went for their usual runs. Elise used that time to take the speeder out for a spin, exploring some new Ardani nook or cranny. She still had so much to see. To memorize.

To savor.

She had been on Arda for nine stellar days, and she couldn't have imagined how fascinating and sensual her new home would be. Everything seemed impossibly bright, clean, and fresh. Arda was as colorful as a painter's palette. New sounds, new smells, and new sensations surprised her every hour. Even the air felt smooth and soothing on her skin. Sometimes she went naked just to savor it, though she still didn't feel comfortable enough to do that outside of Camford.

Of course, Camford was essentially a walled city created for the Tul'Mar family by masons and craftsmen of unsurpassed skill. Camford's weathered stone structure had stood strong for thousands of years. Eight thousand and five years, to be precise. The rooms smelled of light honeysuckle, which Ki called mora-flower, and rose-like blossoms splashed the outer stones with greens, reds, yellows, and different shades of pink. Camford had chambers for chambers, and towers holding towers.

Smiling servants kept the great palace polished and fresh around the clock. There were libraries and pools. Great halls, small halls, round rooms, square rooms, tapestries, murals, sculptures—and surely all the magic mirrors from childhood fairytales hung in some yet-unexplored marble passageway.

Camford had hunting grounds and riding grounds, fields of grain, and fields teeming with incredibly-colored Chimera. Elise had decided Chimeras must be part unicorn, because every time she came close to one, she heard music in her heart.

And Arda itself. God, but Arda had to be something from a dream. Endless blue skies, an orange-yellow sun with a tiny, whiter sun joining it like a child holding a mother's hand—and the mountains. Some thickly wooded, some capped with snow, and others gently rolling and shrouded in mist like the Great Smokies on her former planet.

Earth wasn't remotely interesting to Elise anymore, except for her cousin Georgia. And for that painful problem, Elise had formed a plan.

She piloted the speeder over the forest that surrounded Ki's castle. *Their* castle. And she smiled.

Trees similar to pines, but thicker with branches and sporting blue cones instead of brown, spread beneath her like sea. And she had seen the Western Sea, only that morning. As well as two herds of hideously ugly and hairy white buffalo-looking things the computer identified as fergilla. Many insults now made better sense to Elise.

The speeder, which was roughly the size of an Earth commuter plane with long, hooked wings, could travel anywhere on Arda in under twenty Earth minutes. It moved too fast to comprehend, yet Elise felt like she was cruising air highways in a Cadillac.

The speeder's control panel was so easy to operate—simpler than the switchboard Elise had manned in her mind-numbing government job. Even better, the ship had an endless-fusion power source, seemingly straightforward maintenance, and ample storage for food in the back hold. Elise had stocked it again this morning, careful to keep the provisions hidden in cabinets and under blankets. With luck, Krysta wouldn't notice. And luck didn't have much to do with it, because Elise was nearly ready to go.

She *was* ready, in fact. As of this flight, all she needed was the right moment. When her instinct told her to go.

By Elise's best calculations, and according to the expanse of star charts stored in the speeder's guidance system, she could travel to Earth and back in less than ten stellar days. Twelve tops. She could rescue Georgia from pain, suffering, and a life of endless boredom and loneliness, and be back with her *sha* before that Presentation ceremony he kept talking about.

The speeder was armed with small guns and lasers. Not enough to blow up a skull ship, of course, but enough to get her out of a tight spot and let the ship's incredible engines do the rest. Elise had practiced firing them out over the sea, and done fairly well with her targets. The computer made things easy.

Through innocent questioning in her sessions with Akad, Elise also had determined that space travel posed no special risks during her 140-day pregnancy. Not until the last ten stellar days, anyway, and she was only twenty-five days along. Her stomach had barely begun to swell. Georgia would be on Arda with her by the time the baby was born.

Elise's arrival was still a matter of mystery to the kingdom, since she hadn't been Presented yet. Ki's crew was notoriously tight-lipped about *Astoria*'s travels, and ruthlessly loyal to Ki and Fari. No one would have to know how Georgia got to Arda—except Ki, Fari, and Krysta. And Elise didn't think they would turn her in for breaking the law about interfering with primitive cultures. After all, until a few months ago, Elise *was* a primitive.

Best of all, once Georgia was with her, Elise would be an unburdened primitive. She would be completely happy, and maybe able to bond fully with Ki, share his thoughts and emotions completely. Like a true Ardani mate.

And that was something Elise wanted almost as much as Georgia's rescue—and Lord Gith's eradication from the universe.

Like a seasoned pro, Elise set the speeder on its landing pad, just inside Camford's bailey. Several technicians in black tunics rushed out to help her down, but Krysta beat them to the ladder.

"Hail, sister!" she called, reaching for Elise's hand.

"Good morning." Elise grinned as Krysta helped her over the large first step, kissed her, then hugged her tightly. "I didn't scratch it, I promise."

"Far better than I did in my first month of flying. Come. Breakfast is waiting."

Running like a child at play, Elise followed Krysta into the massive side doors of Camford's great hall. In the dining room, Ki stood and greeted her with a deep, warming kiss. Fari kissed her as well, and servants heaped her plate with pastries, fruit, and deliciously rich cheeses. Elise never had less than three types of juice to choose from, and so far, everything had tasted like food from heaven. Sweet, light, and completely filling. She loved the feel of the new textures on her tongue, and delighted in the familiar, yet strange smells from the plates and kitchens.

Conversation was always cheerful, light, and loving, and this morning was no different. After breakfast, Krysta headed off to see to the Chimera herds for a bit. Ki and Fari announced that they needed to take care of some trading route matters, but Ki promised to join his *shanna* in the early afternoon.

"Go to the libraries," he suggested. "Try the one in the East tower. I think it will please you. Read, as you so love to do, and I will meet you there as soon as I can."

Ki kissed Elise again before he left, making sure she could feel the hard-on in his brown leather breeches.

She gave it a playful tweak. "Don't be too long."

His dark eyes blazed. "Most certainly, I will not."

Elise's heart felt light as she navigated the long castle hallways, relying on the kind gestures and pointing of the servants to find the East tower. As she walked, she knew she should feel guilty about her plot to snatch the speeder and sneak off to Earth, but she didn't. A little worried, maybe, because she didn't want to make Ki angry, or hurt Krysta's feelings.

Georgia was a non-negotiable issue to Ki, though. And it was non-negotiable to Elise, too. This one time, things would have to go her way. She felt sure Ki would understand, once she returned. And if he didn't, Elise felt sure she could persuade him to forgive her.

The East tower library proved to be yet another stunning experience.

The minute Elise entered, she knew the books were much older than the ones in the West, South, and North towers. Even the large, stately leather-like couch and chairs had a look of antiquity, and the walls were covered with murals. Scenes from Arda's magnificent landscape. Striking figures Elise figured for Ki's ancestors. And on the back right wall, shaded from the sun but lit by candles on an altar and two torches in wall brackets, she found the three wild women she had seen in virtually every room on the ship and in the castle.

In this mural, the weird sisters looked more like cats than true females. They were tall and beautiful, like Krysta, yet lighter in color. One was still blondish, while one had long auburn curls, and the third—her hair seemed to change in the flickering light.

Their eyes glimmered silver, like the startling *pa* designs around their eyes. Flames. Yes. Like the ones on Ki's chest, but thinner and more feminine. More...truly feral. And those fangs and claws.

Elise backed up a step.

She gazed at them for a long time, unable to look away. In the odd lighting, the women seemed to dance in their carefully sketched and colored field.

What did this painting mean?

Elise had studied Arda's basic religions, and none had deities like the ones on the library wall. She had looked for the three women in several reference books, but found nothing.

"So, you like that rendering?" Krysta's resonant voice cut through the silence, startling Elise.

"W-What rendering?" Elise glanced at her sister-in-law, who walked slowly to her side in front of the odd mural.

"The *Lorelei*." Krysta slipped her arm around Elise's shoulder. "The wild women. Half Ardani, half primitive. They are said to live in the Camford Forest, guarding Tul'Mar lands, the castle, and those of Tul'Mar blood. No one has ever seen them, but many a drunken traveler has told tales of howlings in the night, or waking with clawed clothing—and intimate scratches."

"I've seen pictures of them before, on the ship and in our room—but I couldn't find them in the books."

Krysta tightened her grip. "They are a Tul'Mar emblem. Like family ghosts."

Elise laughed and snuggled closer to Krysta. She liked being near her sister-in-law. She also liked their almost sexual touching, which still surprised her. Caresses and kisses. Smelling Krysta's minty scent, and feeling her silky skin and satin hair. More and more, Elise thought of asking Ki to invite Krysta to join them one night, but she held back.

That was almost too much. And still, it was fun—and exciting—to consider.

"Our family legend says the *Lorelei* will show themselves one day." Krysta kissed Elise's hair. "To save the Tul'Mar bloodline from certain doom. We are still waiting. For the doom, as well as the saving."

The dancing *Lorelei* caught Elise's attention once more. They were touching each other. Holding hands. The two on the left, the blond and the redhead, had arms linked, even.

I wish I were a wild woman, she thought, forgetting to shield her mind. *Maybe then I would have the courage to really kiss Krysta, and see what it feels like.*

Krysta's light embrace tensed, and Elise realized her mistake. "I—I'm sorry. I know that was—that I—"

"That you what?" Krysta's tone was low as she turned Elise to face her. "That you have interest in me? In touching another woman?"

Elise flushed and nodded.

Krysta eased forward and kissed Elise's forehead with her full, soft lips. "What is wrong with that, sister? Attraction to your husband's same-generation kin is as normal as breathing."

"Not where I come from." Elise knew she had to be glowing in the darkened corner of the library. "I mean, women do have sex with women, but society is very…um, uptight about that."

Krysta's lips brushed Elise again, this time on her left ear. A pleasant chill traveled across Elise's shoulders.

"I do not think I would like Earth much," Krysta said. "Denying the natural, it is bad for health and happiness."

"Mmm-hmm." Elise couldn't form a whole word, because Krysta was kissing her neck. Nibbling the tender flesh between her ear and collarbone, like Ki did, only more gently. First one side, and then the other.

And then Krysta pulled back and locked her midnight gaze on Elise. Their thoughts joined, and Elise felt Krysta's arousal—both emotional, and physical. Different from her husband's, but no less warm. No less passionate.

Elise's heart drummed at the feel of another woman's desire. Another woman's desire *for her.*

Almost instantly, Elise's nipples began to ache. She gave in to her curiosity, imagining Krysta's soft kisses, her tender biting. Elise's whole body vibrated with the images flowing between them. Thoughts of Krysta's tongue exploring her mouth, flicking against her tight nipples, tasting the already wet heat between her legs. Thoughts of learning Krysta's curves and cries. Her sensitive spots. The rich smell of Krysta's sex and excitement.

Slowly, stroking Elise's hair, Krysta leaned down and kissed Elise full on the mouth. Not a fast kiss of greeting, or a tentative kiss of exploration. A deep, slow, and sensual delving.

Elise let out a quiet moan, and pressed herself against Krysta's firm breasts.

Krysta embraced her and kissed her again, longer and sweeter, but then pulled back. "Are you certain you want this? I do not wish for you to be uncomfortable with me."

"I want this," Elise said before her upbringing could get in the way.

"Ki will be along soon." Krysta nodded to the big leather couch across the library, back in the brighter light of day. "Until he arrives, let us talk. And get more comfortable."

Speechless again, Elise followed Krysta to the couch and started to sit down, but Krysta caught her arm. "Undress me first, before we sit. And I will undress you. That much is permissible without Ki. He will be pleased to find us ready, I think."

No doubt. Elise smiled. In many ways, Earth men and Ardani men were alike, after all. She eyed Krysta's form-fitting black body suit, and this time openly stared at her cleavage. Her cheeks were burning, but she reached out and took hold of the zipper between her sister-in-law's full, tempting breasts.

Slowly, Elise eased the zipper down, to Krysta's belly, and lower, until the track ended. Elise felt the soft down of Krysta's lower hair brushing her fingertips, and her hand shook as she turned loose of the zipper. But she didn't move her fingers. The feeling was too exciting.

Bringing her other hand to the divide in Krysta's body suit, Elise slowly lifted her arms, letting her hands feel the way as she pushed upward, opening the suit until Krysta's breasts fell free. With another push upward, Elise removed the suit from Krysta's shoulders, and Krysta slipped her arms out.

The suit fell to Krysta's waist, and once more, Elise allowed herself to stare. Krysta had large breasts, like Georgia's, but her nipples were dark. A rich, brownish red, and the swollen tips were invitingly round and full.

"Do you like what you see?" Krysta whispered.

Elise nodded. She wanted to touch Krysta's breasts. Fasten her mouth on them and suck as Ki had so often done to give Elise exquisite pleasure. But that would have to wait until Ki could share the feelings and sensations.

Damn him. He needs to get here soon!

Krysta grinned. With a slight twist and a graceful step, she shed the rest of the body suit and stood naked before Elise. The hair between her legs was as dark as the hair on her head, and it looked long and achingly soft.

Elise's fingers twitched.

Ki-iii, she groaned in her mind. *Hurry up, would you?*

And then Krysta was undressing Elise, sliding her tunic over her head, and taking her own inventory of what she saw. Her hungry smile conveyed her pleasure, and for a moment, her hand lingered on Elise's belly.

Elise felt a jolt of connection, like she did when Ki touched the child growing inside her. It was comforting, that sensation. A sense of total safety and acceptance, and a deep joining with the Tul'Mars.

Family love.

Krysta moved her hands down, and carefully unlaced Elise's loose breeches. They fell away, and Krysta's eyes roved over the light hair of Elise's triangle.

Elise felt as if Krysta's hands were already teasing and discovering—but they weren't.

Not yet.

With a skillful kick, Krysta sent their clothes away from the couch, and beckoned for Elise to sit down.

When she did, the couch's soft leathery feel doubled Elise's excitement. Her skin slid easily back and forth across the cushion, and it cradled her so comfortably as she gazed at Krysta's sculpted face.

Krysta's eyes never moved from Elise's face, either. Even when she said, "After Ki arrives, while he watches, I want to taste you everywhere."

The words felt like thrusts from Krysta's long, slender fingers, deep in her pussy. Elise's insides quivered, as if Krysta's mouth and hands were already at work. "I bet you taste sweet," she managed to say between furious blushes. "Like the juices at breakfast."

Krysta's breath caught at those words, and Elise smiled. If Ki didn't get here in the next five minutes, she might have to kill him.

"Murder will not be necessary," Ki murmured from the library door as he entered.

Elise felt her heart leap at the sound of her husband's voice, and she smiled at his surprised, interested look. His eyes blazed with joy and arousal as he turned to close them inside the library, and by the time he turned back around, he had already removed his shirt. His cock strained at his breeches, but he removed them quickly as well.

Krysta stood and pointed to a chair a few strides from them. "Sit there, brother. And watch us."

"And no touching," Elise added, standing up beside Krysta. "Us, or yourself."

Ki chuckled, but the throaty sound told Elise the idea pleased him very much. His thoughts reached out and twined with hers, and then she knew just how pleased he was.

So did Krysta, who laughed before turning to Elise and sliding her arm around Elise's shoulder again. "Men are predictable, yes?"

"Definitely." Elise leaned into Krysta's embrace, and then they were body to body, and kissing.

Ki's sharp intake of breath made them both smile, and urged them on. Elise's hands found Krysta's nipples and let them rub her palms during the next kiss. She kneaded them gently, finding a sudden comfort in knowing what pleased women. After all, she was a woman, and she knew what pleased her.

Krysta's warm thoughts and deep moans bolstered her confidence. Slowly, but deliberately, Krysta began her own explorations. First she stroked Elise's cheeks and hair as they kissed. Then her shoulders, her breasts, and her nipples.

Just the right pressure, and perfect timing.

Elise gasped, and Ki groaned. The sound of his desire doubled her wetness as Krysta lowered her head and suckled one breast, and then the other. Her woman's lips were softer than Ki's, but her mouth felt just as eager

"So good," Elise whispered.

Krysta sighed and raised her head, and Elise took her turn, welcoming Krysta's large, dark nipple into her mouth. Her own breasts twinged as Krysta let out soft moans. Elise could feel Krysta's pleasure, and Ki's doubling want, and she knew so intimately what it felt like to have her own nipples kneaded and touched—it was intoxicating. Almost overwhelming.

Ki's thoughts eased back a step, as did Krysta's. They were being careful not to override Elise's brain and knock her out again.

Good thing, because as Elise knelt to taste Krysta's pussy for the first time, she thought she might faint.

You do not have to—Krysta began, but Elise pulled Krysta's hips forward and buried her face and mouth in the wispy, silken hair. At the same time, she eased her hand between Krysta's legs and played in the damp, swollen slit.

Yes. She tasted like nectar. Not too sweet, and not salty. Just rich and wet, like hidden juice. Letting her fingers ease inside Krysta, she ached at the warmth, the feeling of dipping into a velvet well.

Why should men have all this fun?

Krysta's back arched, and she thrust herself against Elise's tongue. "Sweet suns in the sky…"

Elise's tongue found the swollen clit she had been seeking, and she knew exactly what to do. Keeping hold of one hip with her free hand, she pulled Krysta even closer. The other hand she kept busy in the depths of Krysta's slit. At first she pumped with slow ease, but as Krysta's muscles tensed, Elise moved her hand harder and faster.

Ki's groaning grew louder, matching his sister's guttural purrs. Krysta's hips bucked, and she buried her hands in Elise's hair, pulling hard.

In the next second, Krysta came violently, jamming herself into Elise's mouth with wracking tremors. Elise felt Krysta's hot walls squeeze against her fingers again and again, keeping time with her deep, satisfied shivers.

When the last contractions subsided, Elise eased her hand from Krysta's depths and stood. Her knees were shaking.

Krysta, however, seemed more energized than ever. She grabbed Elise and pulled her into a fierce kiss. The smell of Krysta's sweet juice lingered between their lips, and Krysta turned Elise and sat her down on the couch, facing Ki.

Elise took in his hooded eyes. His straining cock.

As instructed, he had his hands firmly on the chair arms, holding on for dear life.

Krysta kissed Elise again and again, cupping her breasts and squeezing, then moving her mouth down Elise's neck to her breasts. Her tongue worked against Elise's hard, aching nipples, and her hands stroked Elise's sides.

Elise glanced down, watching Krysta suck her breasts.

Oh, God, but that was almost unbearable.

She was so close to coming she could barely stand it. So was Ki. Elise could feel his near-orgasm throbbing through her thoughts.

Krysta eased her mouth down again, brushing her lips over Elise's slightly swollen belly. Elise ran her fingers through Krysta's hair, resisting an urge to cram the woman's face between her legs.

And then she didn't have to fight the urge any longer.

Krysta took Elise's swollen clit in her mouth and sucked it, just as she had nursed Elise's breasts. Drinking her. Milking and flicking her warm tongue over Elise's most sensitive spot even as she slipped her fingers into Elise's pussy, seemingly to her very core.

The sensation swallowed Elise whole, and she bowed forward, screaming with the force of her orgasm. As she closed her eyes, she saw Ki grip the chair arms so tightly they seemed to melt in his powerful grasp.

Ki leaped to his feet before Elise settled from her explosion.

Sensing his presence behind her, Krysta slid gracefully aside. She then climbed nimbly behind Elise on the couch and cradled his *shanna*. A chair of flesh, kneading Elise's breasts and raising Elise's hips to meet Ki's pulsing cock.

Elise's eyes never opened, so lost she was in the fullness of her pleasure. Her legs splayed wide as Ki grabbed them, and she cried out again and again as he entered her quim.

"Yes. God, yes!" She writhed as Ki pumped and Krysta pinched her nipples without mercy.

The tight, liquid heat of Elise's slit, the sound of his frenzied pounding into her wet quim, and the rustle of Elise's backside rubbing Krysta's wet sex drove Ki over the top in a matter of seconds. He tightened like cordwood.

Curling backward, he lifted Elise nearly off the couch. Krysta held her firmly, suspended between them. Elise's face was a study in rapture as her body stretched to its full length. She was fully at his mercy, and fully trusting. Her legs squeezed against his hips.

Ki paused for a moment and gazed at her closed eyes, her swollen peaks, the tinge of red in her cheeks and around her mound—she was beyond beautiful.

Elise moaned and came with him as he slammed into her slit one final time, emptying himself like a boiling flask. Krysta's orgasm, wrought from a few well-placed strokes from her own fingers, blended with theirs as they dropped from the pinnacle to the soft, sweet plains of exhaustion.

Afterwards, the three of them lay in a heap on the floor.

Elise alternately kissed Ki, then Krysta as she drifted in and out of sleep, and as they drifted in and out of long afternoon of lovemaking. Ki never touched his sister in a sexual way, of course, as such was not custom. Krysta was there for Elise's pleasure, and pleasure Elise they did.

Several times, Ki worried that the psi connections might harm his *shanna* again, but Krysta always seemed to know when to ease back. And she had a talent for reaching Ki's thoughts and pulling him back with her. Just a step. Like a shadowdance. As subtle and graceful as the cavorting *Lorelei* on the back wall.

The wild women of legend could scarcely hold a candle to Elise. Of that, Ki felt certain.

He also felt guilt, for not being able to grant the one wish she had laid before him: the retrieval of her kin from Earth.

How he wished he could grant her pleadings, but he could not. He simply could not.

Quickly, Ki moved from guilt to worry over Lord Gith, the next actions of the Council, and the OrTans in general. His instincts bothered him. He sensed something amiss, but he could not define it. And that maddened him.

Gazing at Elise and his sleeping sister, the desire to defend them nearly overwhelmed him. He would kill any man or beast who so much as breathed foul air in their direction.

Madness. Love is a madness. The truest truth I have ever heard spoken.

Absorbing his disquiet, Elise stirred and grumbled in her slumber. Krysta's arm flopped across Elise's belly, and she, too, fussed from her dreams. Ki forced his thoughts into compliance, and set aside concerns of war long enough to kiss his *shanna*'s damp brow.

"Are you leaving?" she murmured, reaching down to stroke his well-used cock.

"Fari has need of my time." He closed his eyes, enjoying the soft squeezing from her fingers.

"I have need of you, inside me. Once more. Please, just once more."

What could Ki do but oblige such an invitation?

After all, Elise's mouth was already taking him in, sucking him to hardness again. And Krysta had already moved between his *shanna*'s open thighs. It would take but a few more stellar minutes for the three of them to take one last pleasure…

Three long hours later, Ki faced Fari in the war room. His brother was in foul temper, and Ki could scarcely blame him. Still, he did not regret his stolen time, or the effort it took to leave Elise with Krysta, limp in slumber on the library floor. Elise's sweet musk hung about his face, hands, and loins, and the fragrance alone was enough to keep part of Ki's thoughts on the night yet to arrive.

"Your thoughts had best turn to these threats." Fari smacked a hand on a star chart spread on the war room table.

With force of will, Ki tore his thoughts from the feel of his *shanna*'s warm mouth and warmer quim. He glanced down at Fari's pointing finger, and immediately saw the problem.

The OrTan fleet had changed positions. The models of their foul battle skulls had been bunched and moved closer to Arda.

Was this what my instincts tried to tell me, but a few hours ago?

"Yes," Fari hissed. "Our enemy is moving. Our scouts reported mass flights beginning almost four stellar hours ago. I called for you over and over, but you did not answer. Our sister was unresponsive as well."

Ki shrugged an apology. His mind had cleared as if icewinds had blown through his brain, and he was not interested in trading barbs or recriminations.

Fari, however, let out a long growl. "Will the Sailmaster and the captain of the Home Guard be hard at coupling when the hounds arrive at our very gates?"

"You cannot think they will attack us directly." Ki shook his head. "It would be suicide."

"Not if the Council throws force behind them." Fari gestured to another group of ships, varied and larger than the skulls. "The Council force is moving as well. On an intercept course. Whether they mean to join or intervene, we do not know."

Ki felt a numb chill spread through his chest. "The case is yet to be heard. The Council would not seek to act—"

Fari interrupted him with a snort. "They would if Gith has unknown allies. Or if he favored the right palms with the right currencies or pleasures."

Surely this had been the source of his troubled mind. Ki knew now—though his instinct yet dug at him—that this extra threat must have been what bothered him so. His sharp eyes took in the corners and players on the map. Even at good speed, and assuming the worst, the combined force would reach Arda in ten stellar days. Nine if they caught the blessing of moon winds and slipstreams.

"Then our choices are few," Ki said in a low voice, as if Elise might hear him and wake frightened without his comfort. "Send word to our surest allies. I will dispatch Krysta and the Guard to the skies immediately, to patrol for vanguards and saboteurs."

Fari nodded. His expression remained tense, but his relief at Ki's focus was obvious.

Ki's anger mounted as he stared at the ships littering the map beside his brother's hand. "And send Akad to my chambers immediately. Tell the people they will meet Elise Tul'Mar at Solstyce. When the moon rises. Afterward, we will announce the threat, and make ready the ground defenses."

Fari's frown deepened. "That is nine stellar days, brother. How can Elise be ready to handle *pa* so soon?"

"Because she has no choice." Ki clenched his fists. "She is strong-minded and wise. She will find a way."

"May you be as right as you have ever been. Our lives depend on it." Fari turned away and stalked out of the war room.

Ki watched him go, knowing the abruptness indicated no disrespect. His brother was afraid. For the planet, and for Elise, and for Ki's unborn daughter.

Growling, Ki shunned his own fears like a plague. The next days would pass in a blur. Too much preparation, too fast, but it had to be done.

Filled with new energy and purpose, Ki strode out of the castle's stronghold and back toward the library. He intended to wake Krysta and get her on her way—but she met him on the run before he reached the main hall.

Her pale face, rumpled hair, and half-dressed state caught him by surprise. Despite her confidence and bluster, Krysta did not usually fly about the castle in disarray. Fari must have gotten word to her.

And yet, the gnawing in his gut increased.

Threat. Wrong. Trouble. Terrible trouble.

Krysta's thoughts? His own instincts?

"You heard, then?" Ki asked, catching her by the shoulders.

"What?" Krysta's breath came in short gasps. Tears spilled down her cheeks, further unsettling Ki.

"About the OrTans? The Council?" Ki gave Krysta a shake. "Speak. What is it?"

For a moment, Krysta said nothing. She looked as if the very thought of words pained her. Shaking, she at last opened her mouth, and uttered the last thing Ki expected to hear.

"Elise is gone, brother."

"Gone where?" His mind both understood and rejected Krysta's message at once. It was not possible. That could not be.

"Home. To Earth." Krysta thrust a rumpled paper toward him. "She left you, Ki. She left you!"

Mouth open, speechless, Ki snatched the paper and stared at it. At first, he could not comprehend the writing, not until he battled back waves of dread and forced his brain to cooperate.

"No." He closed the paper, then opened it again. It held his eyes like a magical force, even as his thoughts raced to solutions and rejected them.

Fari had no doubt put out the announcement of the Presentation. It was too late to call it back now. And even if they flew after Elise at top speed, they would never reach her in time. The enemies, approaching Arda—a flight of speeders or a frigate pursuing Elise might alert the monsters. Might lead them straight to his *shanna* and their helpless, growing babe.

Once more, he stared at the paper, shaking his head.

Once more, Ki Tul'Mar read his doom, written in his true love's neat penmanship.

Dear Ki,

I'm sorry to do this, but I think you know I have to go. Georgia is my family, too, and I need her with me. Don't worry, and don't come after me, and please, try not to be too angry. I'll be back before you know it.

Always your beloved,

Elise

Chapter 10

Elise tapped her fingers on the speeder's companel. Her chest tightened, and her brain literally ached.

She had gotten away clean from Arda. The sky patrol hadn't even attempted to contact her, since she was in Krysta's speeder. She should have been glad, but instead, she felt like she had flown off and forgotten her heart.

Ki. I've gotten so used to his thoughts, his energy close by. It's so quiet without him. So…empty.

"Just a few days," she whispered against the thrum of the engines. "He'll be mad, but he'll forgive me."

Won't he? Christ. What if he doesn't?

Visions of Ki's dark hair and eyes flashed through Elise's mind as she gazed into the black depths of space. Her hand rested on her belly, gently rubbing the spot where her daughter nestled inside, sleeping at the moment. She could sense the baby, just as she had learned to sense Ki. Akad had told her that somewhere around her hundredth day of gestation, she would begin to hear her daughter's thoughts.

For now, though, everything seemed quiet and still. Too quiet, too still.

The stars watched her without blinking. Maybe they thought Elise was ungrateful, because they had granted almost every wish she had ever whispered in their direction—and here she was, possibly throwing away their hard work.

"I have to do this," she told the stars and her daughter. "I can't live happily ever after knowing Georgia's all alone. She would never go to paradise and leave me behind. She would find a way."

Calling up the star charts on the speeder's computer, Elise studied her routes. The advanced Ardani technology would warn her of obstacles, debris, anomalies—even correct for them. Everything was preprogrammed and considered.

At least Elise hoped so.

She had learned much in the last week or so, but she knew she was no ace navigator, pilot, or master of clandestine activity. Her big secret plan consisted of sneaking off from Arda, flying straight to Earth as fast as she could, landing the speeder on top of her old apartment complex in Nashville (there was room—please, let there be enough room), grabbing Georgia, and zooming straight home to her husband.

Because Arda was Elise's home now, and she already missed Ki so badly she wanted to cry. She missed the castle, the libraries, the mountains, the clouds, the Chimera—everything. And Krysta and Fari, too.

Without thinking, Elise reached up and kneaded her breasts through the soft tunic. The tips still felt tender from her lovemaking with Ki and Krysta, and she slipped her hands beneath her long shirt. When her fingers found the hardened flesh of her nipples, she let out a sigh. Half pleasure and excitement, half longing.

At the moment, she wanted five or six uninterrupted days and nights with Ki. She wanted to be on her back, legs spread, taking his full cock as hard as he could give it to her. Or on her knees, feeling him pound into her from behind. Elise rubbed the ends of her nipples and groaned.

His mouth felt so good on her lips, her breasts, her skin and pussy. His cock felt so perfect planted inside her. Elise reached down and toyed with her clit to relieve the ache, then slipped her fingers back, inside, where she wanted Ki. Her body was made for him, and his body for her. Touching his thoughts, knowing his heart, being consumed in his passion—loving him had come so easily, despite the odd beginnings.

As the speeder hurtled toward Earth, deftly skirting solar systems and dodging asteroids, Elise leaned over the com-panel. Her nipples brushed control switches as she stroked her swollen clit and dreamed of Ki. His warm presence. His throbbing, hot cock. The hard muscles of his chest, and the swirling silver of his *pa*-mark. The look of keen pleasure on Ki's face as Fari used his mouth to bring her to climax. The desire raging through Ki as Krysta gently sucked Elise to new heights of discovery.

Everything Elise shared with Fari and Krysta only brought Ki closer to her. It felt so right and natural. The speeder careened ahead, and so did Elise's fingers. Flying now, hammering against her pulsing clit until she came with a loud, releasing scream. Knobs scraped her nipples. The cool metal floor grounded her feet, and her knees shook until she sat down.

Stripping off her tunic, she started over. Lying naked in deep space, trusting the ship to see her safely through, she squeezed her breasts, then thrust her fingers in and out of her wet pussy. Orgasm after orgasm, she called Ki's name and thrashed. Completely unashamed. Wild with the freedom, until she lay gasping and half-asleep on the speeder's small deck.

Her last thought as she drifted to sleep was of her mate. How he might like to watch what she had just done. And how she wanted to show him, as soon as she got back to Arda.

* * * * *

Elise's thoughts and emotions carried to Ki as he lay unclothed and alone in his bed. The bed he should be sharing with his wife. His mast ached and swelled, and he relieved the pressure time and again with his own hands. It did not matter. In moments, he would gather another whiff of Elise's sensations, and harden all over again.

She thinks of me as she climaxes, just as she did the day I found her. Her heart is true to me. And yet she carves my soul to bits.

Under the circumstances, he could certainly ask any willing woman to meet his need. No doubt there would be many volunteers among the servants, or among the many citizens or rescues-becoming-citizens on Arda. Custom and tradition allowed a husband or wife to satiate sexual desire in the physical absence of their mate—but most soul's mates had no interest in doing this. Ki understood that now. He wanted only Elise's touch. Only her hot, sweet sheath around his flesh.

It had been mere hours since he plumbed her hot depths, but it felt like years. And now, her trace-thoughts grew ever more distant as she sped out of his life. Out of their life. He would likely never see her again. Even if Elise survived her trip, Ki Tul'Mar would likely be dead by the time she returned.

It was the law. There was little Ki could do, even though he knew—and Fari and Krysta knew, especially now—that his *shanna* had not left him in love or spirit. Only in body. And she planned to return with due speed. Still, the Presentation announcement had been made, and there was no taking it back now. Another statement of illness would prompt a medical evaluation, as per provisions of Ardani custom—to avoid the endless hiding of a Sailmaster's abandonment. There would be talk. Already begun, no doubt.

Ki imagined he could smell the musk of Elise's sweet nectar still on his face, his fingers. And perhaps he could. A soul's mate could sense their beloved's presence at great distance. And after long stretches of time.

Why did I deny her the one request she made?

But Ki knew he could not violate the law at will. He was a Sailmaster, not a god. Galactic laws of non-interference applied to him, too.

I should have found a way.

A knock rattled him from his trance, and he groaned. "Please. Leave me in peace."

The chamber door opened despite his request, and Fari and Krysta entered. Akad was close behind.

Ki did not bother covering himself, or his miserable, insatiable cock.

The priest approached him warily, expecting violence. Madness. And Ki felt insane—but insanely sad. His anger had left him like a spent wind. All sails, inside and outside the Sailmaster, had gone flat.

"Sire." Akad extended a vial. "This may relieve your physical pain, at least for a time."

Ki turned his head to the far wall.

"Leave it." Krysta sighed. "Thank you, Akad. And trust this stubborn fergilla to us."

Footsteps padded across stone, and the chamber door closed with a quiet thump.

"Take the medicine," Fari said.

Ki ignored him.

"Consume it, or we will pour it down your throat." Fari tried to sound furious, but succeeded only in communicating his fear. "You cannot fight the both of us."

"Do not tempt me," Ki growled.

The next he knew, Fari and Krysta had him pinned, and his oh-so-gentle female sibling pried his lips open, dumped the potion in his mouth, then pinched his nose to ensure his swallow. The liquid burned his throat as it dove toward his belly, untying at least a few of the knots in his groin.

After a moment, his thoughts cleared a little, and the pain of separation from Elise waned. At least the physical pain.

"Damn stubborn fool." Fari rolled off the bed. He staggered as he walked, and Ki realized his brother must have taken—or been forced to take—a dose of the same medicine. Krysta also seemed unusually supple, and her eye-centers were pinpoints in the room's grayish light.

"Do you see now that you should have told her about the Law of Keeping?" Krysta stroked Ki's forehead. Tears appeared on her cheeks, as if blown there by a sudden breeze. "You should have trusted her heart, and yours."

Ki knew his sullen silence was as good as agreement, but he did not feel like assenting out loud. After all, he would pay price enough for his folly.

"We will not let you die." Fari moved to the sill of the back window. "We will explain. Or fight. Or find some diversion."

Ki tried to speak, found his lips nerveless, then recovered his muscle control enough to say, "That has been tried in the past. Always with ill result, for the Sailmaster in question, and for Arda. I will not have my honor or my legacy sullied by cowardice."

At this, Krysta got up with a sharp grunt. "No. As usual, you would prefer rash foolishness to be your trademark."

"He did not teach her to fly a speeder," Fari snapped.

"We all taught her to fly," Ki mumbled. "And she loves us. She has gone to get the one missing member of her heart's family. No more or less than we would have done. No more or less than we *should* have done."

For almost a stellar hour afterward, Ki argued with Krysta and Fari about possible solutions to the dilemma, but they could find none. At last, in exasperation, he lay back on his pillows. "Let us work from the other end. Assuming my death instead of preventing it for a moment."

"No." Fari threw himself on the bed beside Ki, but kept his distance. He stared at the ceiling, gripping the sheets in his fists. "I will not hear that."

"Nor will I," Krysta agreed.

Ki frowned. "Hear me this far, at least. I want Elise returned with her sister of choice. I want my daughter protected. Perhaps if we work on those problems, the clear way out of my execution will become apparent."

Fari and Krysta grew silent, which was, for them, a tacit agreement.

Relief swept over Ki. He no more believed he would escape death than he believed Fari truly bedded fergilla beasts, but for the moment, the focus of the group was where he chose for it to be. On Elise. On seeing his *shanna,* his precious baby, and his *shanna*'s beloved relative safely home to Arda.

* * * * *

Five stellar days after her "escape" from Arda, five impossibly long days full of tears, fitful sleep, and far too much self-gratification (which became less gratifying each time), Elise Ashton Tul'Mar swept into orbit around Earth.

Anti-detection shielding automatically deployed around the speeder. She felt a sense of triumph as the computer informed her the shielding was functioning well. And then she felt nothing but worry.

What if she rammed a skyscraper? Crashed into the Grand Canyon?

"Knock it off."

She sighed.

Talking to herself had become a bad habit, especially since she reached Pluto. Nerves, she guessed. The baby—now she could speak to the baby without a moment's hesitation.

"We're off to fetch Auntie Georgia," Elise murmured. "Are you with me?"

Thankfully, the baby didn't offer a comment.

Carefully working the buttons and steering switch, Elise eased the speeder into the atmosphere. Unlike rockets on TV, the speeder didn't burn or rattle. It floated, almost like a feather. The descent felt like a slightly fast elevator ride through rocks, dust, and buffeting currents.

And then Elise saw pinkish evening sky, and nothing but ocean below. The speeder didn't even leave a shadow on the whitecaps.

Using the Earth geocharts available in the computer banks, Elise pinpointed her position in the Atlantic, programmed coordinates for Nashville, and eased forward at the speed of roughly four times that of a Concord jet.

The U.S. coastline sprang into view, and Elise crossed over North Carolina's Outer Banks. Right over the Albemarle Sound and Kitty Hawk island itself. The misty slopes of the Smoky Mountains rose and fell beneath Elise's wings, and then the ship slowed, and slowed again.

She coasted into the Nashville area just ahead of sunset. The gray-blue sky hosted fat clouds, and Elise could almost feel the heat shimmering toward the speeder. Using the hand-steering knob, which felt a lot like a computer mouse, Elise took herself around Nashville's tall, spikey "Batman building", down the main streets of Broadway and then West End, and to the top of her old haunt, Crestview Village.

"Oh, thank God." The roof looked wide enough and strong enough to hold the speeder.

Elise tapped the descent panel, cutting the engines back and easing down, down, and down onto the pebble-covered flat expanse.

Dockers deployed with a soft thunk, and the speeder turned itself off, keeping anti-detection shields at full power.

Elise's heart rapped in her throat. "I did it. I actually flew a spaceship from Arda to Earth. Okay, well, it basically flew itself, but I did it!"

Georgia was here, or she soon would be. Just yards away. Mere feet, instead of solar systems.

Elise scrambled out of the speeder, and her breath caught hard in her throat.

God, but the air smelled *awful*. Like smoke and burning trash.

Her lungs rebelled. She coughed, glanced around for the fire—then realized the odor must be from pollution. The normal clutter of Earth's air, so totally unlike the fresh, clean breezes of Arda.

Regaining her mental balance, Elise forced her breathing to behave. A quick scan of the area told her no one seemed to have a vantage point on Crestview's roof, and no one seemed to notice a woman walking into view out of thin air.

Hand on her belly, as if to protect her baby, Elise hurried toward the roof door.

And of course, found it locked.

"Damn it." She rattled the handle, willing it to turn. The knob gave a loud pop and crumbled in Elise's hand.

Creaking a protest, the metal door swung open.

Ooooops. Elise dropped the pulverized knob. *I guess my psi power is active on Earth, too. I thought it only worked in space.*

The stairs from Crestview's roof were dark and dusty, but Elise ran down them without caring. Five flights, from the roof to stairwell eleven—she reached Georgia's floor in only a minute.

This time, she directed gentle but firm thoughts toward the locked door's mechanism. It popped open without exploding, and Elise smiled.

One door left to Georgia, and that one might open with a knock.

Elise strode down the hall to Georgia's apartment. Her mouth ran dry with excitement, and her hand shook as she rapped on the red painted wood.

For a moment, no sound came from the apartment.

Oh, no. What if she's not home? Elise chewed her lip—and then locks clacked, and the door swung wide to reveal Georgia. Her red hair looked wild and rumpled, and her face seemed flushed, like she just woke up. White blouse, blue jean shorts, and a very startled, very thrilled expression—yep, all Georgia, classic-style.

"Oh, my God." Georgia grabbed Elise and smothered her with a hug. Her neck smelled like roses. "Oh, my God! Oh, my GOD! Where have you been? Jesus H. Christ on a creaking crutch! You scared me to death."

"I'm so sorry. And I'm so glad to see you!" Elise stepped inside Georgia's apartment. "Is anyone here?"

"No. Why?" Georgia shut the door behind them. "Is the CIA on your tail or something?"

Chills ran up and down Elise's spine. "No. At least, I don't think so."

Georgia managed to arch one eyebrow, even as she wiped away an obvious tear. "Okay, Miss Mystery. Start talking. Where in the living hell have you been?"

Elise took a deep breath and reached for Georgia's hands. Her cousin's fingers felt warm and welcome in her palms, and yet, when Elise opened her mouth, nothing came out but a sigh.

"Another hug," Elise whispered. "Then we'll talk."

* * * * *

Ki Tul'Mar sensed it when Elise located her cousin on Earth. A sudden stab of well-being. Of joy. Unfortunately, he could not share the emotion then, or now, four stellar days later.

The OrTan fleet was speeding toward Arda, and the Galactic Council forces had joined the massive flotilla. Word had filtered from sources all through the universes that Lord Gith had indeed bribed and persuaded the Council to bend to his viewpoint. The Council had agreed to hear Gith's complaint on Arda, to facilitate the return of Elise to OrTan control at the first possible moment.

The "show of force" was to keep Arda from resisting, once the legalities were established.

Arda, of course, would not be so easily forced into compliance. Krysta and the Home Guard had deployed over key planetary areas, and the bulk of Arda's Fleet set sail with Fari at *Astoria*'s helm. By design, the Fleet would intercept all forces, allowing only the Galactic Council flagship through to Arda. Krysta's speeders would handle any stray vessels.

In most campaigns, Ki would have been on his ship, spearheading the defensive wall. However, in this most rare of times, when Arda herself came under threat, the Sailmaster had but one place to be.

In the war room, on a silken cushion, lending the might of his psi power to each and every sail in the Fleet.

Ki could feel each of his frigates like energy on his skin. He whispered to the *pa* coating sail and board, and to the *pa* protecting and coating so many key structures on Arda.

Hold, he urged. *Join. Hold. Join. Hold.*

And the *pa* answered its master, not with words, but by thriving. Growing stronger and more powerful with each passing stellar hour.

Ki's staff tended his meager needs, and the few times he made eye contact with one of the servants, he noticed how they looked away. To the walls. To their feet.

They know, he realized. *They know my shanna has left me. That I am a dead man, as of moonrise this very evening.*

War would not put off or delay Ki's sentence. Once the people knew the truth, Akad and the other priests would do their duty.

Until that moment, Ki would do *his* duty. He hoped at least to contribute to Arda's victory, and ultimately, to the safety of his mate and child.

The execution would be swift, though not painless. Fari would become Sailmaster immediately, and put for Arda and Camford as soon as battle conditions allowed. This the brothers had resolved, through much shouting and strain. Krysta had not been included in the plans, as she never would have agreed.

At that moment, she was hurtling about the planet, keeping her surface defense troops organized and scanning for Elise's return. It was up to Krysta to intercept Elise and see her safely through the Fleet battle lines—and to get her off of Arda if the legal case or military struggles went poorly.

Ki could sense the approach of darkness as he meditated. Big sun and little sister waned into the western sky as he sat, ticking time with his heartbeats and breath.

Shortly, there came a rustling and coughing before him. As if a great party had entered, but felt loathe to disturb him.

The priests had arrived for the Presentation.

Ki kept his eyes closed, but his hyperaware mind took in the scene.

Akad stood in front, clothed in white and purple robes. The high priest's expression was one of horror and dread. Four lesser priests in black robes accompanied him, and with them, a priest in red waited—in obvious shock. The *Ord'pa*. A ceremonial executioner. Double-axe already in hand.

Little did the man realize he would play more than a role this night.

In halting high words, Akad begged pardon for his interruption, then asked Ki to surrender his mate for evaluation and presentation.

Forcing his thoughts steady, still giving his full mind to the sails, Ki gave the required, though completely unexpected response.

"Shanna Ki Tul'Mar ist onden."

Ki Tul'Mar's mate has departed.

The red-robed priest swayed in place. Murmuring broke out amongst the party, and Akad wavered on his feet.

"Your Majesty, I—I do not—I cannot—what—"

"You will do your duty, priest." Ki's voice was a growl. "Leave me here as long as the law allows, so that I might assist the Fleet. At the appointed moment, I will accompany you to the Tuscan Platform." He opened his eyes and cut them to the *Ord'pa,* who nearly dropped his ceremonial axe. "Peacefully."

For now.

Silence filled the chamber as Akad gave thought to his next words. Ki heard the priest's sigh, and then, "Bekor. Hie and notify the people."

Clothing rustled, and the chamber door opened, then closed.

Akad's next words spilled out in a rush. "Ki Tul'Mar, you are under arrest for failure to meet the provisions of the Law of Keeping. At moonrise, you will journey with us to the Tuscan clearing, whereupon you face the known consequences of your failure."

Ki grunted his assent. His heart felt heavy in his chest, but his mind remained engaged with the needs of the Fleet—and at some level, the needs of his beautiful *shanna.*

Beloved. She could not hear him, he knew, but he had to try. *Know that my heart was yours. Always, and forever. Be strong for our daughter. Dora, shanna. Dora!*

Chapter 11

"You've changed so much." Georgia stroked Elise's loose hair as they stood side by side and stared into the outer reaches of space. The speeder pelted through clouds of dust, around tumbling asteroids, and through the rocky paths of comets. "I can't believe how relaxed you look. How happy."

Elise smiled. Georgia's green eyes were wide in the front window reflection, as they had been since Elise first explained where she had been—and where she wanted Georgia to go. Georgia hadn't hesitated. She hadn't even packed much. Just one small bag of keepsakes, and a few outfits, though Elise had assured her she would prefer the soft, sensual Ardani fabrics.

"You'll love it on Arda," Elise murmured. "And I know you'll find some hunk of a warrior and live in a dream, just like I've been doing."

Georgia's laughter brightened the small deck. "Well, how about I stay at this fabulous castle you keep describing, and meet your hunk first? One step at a time."

"Ki will love you, I know." Elise's eyes traveled to Georgia's ample bosom, despite her best efforts to behave. *He'll love every inch of you. If you don't kill me over this one teeny cultural detail I left out...*

Man, but she was horny. Having Georgia's warm beauty beside her felt so right and perfect, like a piece of her heart had been healed. All Elise could think of was sharing her joy with Ki, connecting with his thoughts fully and completely, giving herself to him in hours of splendid, soul-filling sex. And finally hearing Georgia's cry of ecstasy when Ki made her come, too.

Share and share alike.

Elise already knew from Georgia's comments and thoughts that Georgia wouldn't be too shocked by Ardani customs. In fact, she'd probably be thrilled.

But like Georgia said, one step at a time.

First, finish the journey back to their new home. Next, get the speeder on the ground, and after that, throw herself into Ki's hopefully merciful arms.

"You really miss him, don't you?" Georgia's grin glittered in her reflection.

Elise turned and kissed the side of Georgia's head. "Like breath. I've been away from him less than ten stellar days, and I feel like it's been a century. When I get back—as soon as he speaks to me again—I'm jumping his bones and keeping him busy for at least a week."

"Mmmm." Georgia's grin widened. "And during that time, what am I supposed to do?"

"Oh, I'm sure we'll think of something." Elise coughed. "I think we're still ahead of schedule. The computer keeps registering something about stellar winds, and the ships hull—I don't know. It's like it keeps cleaning itself and moving faster."

"Maybe this little ship is like a horse. You know—hurrying when it sees the barn." Georgia broke away from Elise and went to a side portal. "I keep thinking this'll get boring in a second, but it doesn't. Not even after nearly a week."

"Stellar days," Elise corrected. "Four. Almost five since we left Earth. We should be heading into the Ardani system in a few hours, or maybe sooner. We're moving so much faster on the way home. That estimate clock has changed five times since I've been looking."

"What's that, over there?" Georgia pointed out her window. "All those bright things—and those other big dark things? They're all in straight lines, and they don't look like asteroids."

Elise joined Georgia, at first more interested in the scent of apples and cinnamon in Georgia's hair than the direction in which her cousin was pointing—but there was something odd on the horizon, to the right. Elise hurried to the other side of the ship. The same weird shadows and shapes appeared out the left window, too.

Flashes of silver and streaks of black emerged directly in front of them as well.

A red light blinked on the com-panel. When Elise checked the screen, it noted, *Visibility deflector employed.*

"Visibility deflector?" She felt a squeeze in her chest.

"Something's wrong." Georgia backed away from the portal. "My instinct's bothering me. Elise—what's going on?"

Elise's mouth went desert-dry. "I don't know. I didn't see anything like this—oh, God."

One of the dark shapes in front of the speeder had started to grow. Except it wasn't growing. It was coming closer. When Elise glanced at the com-panel to see if the computers had identified the obstacle, her knees wobbled.

The computer screen flashed green, detailed pictures of an OrTan skull ship. Different perspectives. Best shooting ranges.

"We've got real trouble," Elise told Georgia in a shaky voice. "Go to the back. I'll try to handle it, okay?"

"What are you going to do?"

Elise's fingers trembled over the weapons controls as the skull ship bore down on them. "I don't know. Just get down. Please!"

A soft alarm bell rang. Elise jumped. Her heart picked up the alarm's beat. The computer screen showed the skull's shrinking distance to the speeder. From behind her, Georgia's shallow, panicked breathing doubled Elise's terror.

Why now? Damn! I can't believe this is happening.

Her mind filled with visions of Lord Gith and his alligator balls. What if they blew the speeder out of space? Or worse, boarded it and took them hostage?

Could she reach Ki or someone on Arda if she tried?

Squeaking with frustration, she pushed a communication beacon. Nothing happened.

Out of range, the computer noted.

And still, the skull closed on them.

Elise felt totally exposed and vulnerable. She wished her soft tunic would turn into chain mail, but no luck.

I can't believe I did this. What was I thinking?

"Christ. I'm going to have to shoot at it." Her words sounded strangled in the quiet air.

The speeder's automatic systems attempted a few basic maneuvers to avoid the OrTan slaver, but to no avail. It shuddered once, then grew still.

Elise studied the diagrams of the big ship, and her speeder's weapon controls. She felt like she was about to fire on a whale with a few barroom darts.

"It's stopping," Georgia whispered.

Elise glanced up.

The massive skull eased to a halt.

It was so large Elise couldn't see it all through the viewing window. Her entire speeder would fit in one of the glowing holes that might be eyes, or a nose, or a toothy, grinning mouth.

If Gith was inside, the bastard was probably laughing. Elise wished she had thought to bring a knife. A sword. Anything at all.

For a moment, she stood frozen, and then her hands found her belly. Through the cloth and the thin walls of her skin, she felt her daughter's heartbeat. And she sensed Georgia's, too, blending with her own.

Ki was just a few stellar hours away. One, in fact, according to the estimate clock.

No way would she give up without a battle. No way.

Grinding her teeth, Elise programmed the firing coordinates the computer recommended. She hesitated over the firing control.

One of the skull's eyes winked.

BOOM!

The speeder rocked so hard Elise flew backward. She crashed to the metal floor, taking Georgia with her. Hissing noises broke out over her head, and for a long second, she couldn't breathe.

Then air seemed to rush through the compartment again. Elise gasped, filling her lungs.

"There's a hole in the roof!" Georgia struggled up and pulled Elise to her feet. "Do something. Blow that nasty ship up!"

Elise stared at the gaping hole in the speeder's ceiling panel. She could see stars—and a silvery sheen.

Pa. The *pa* coating the ship had sealed the breach.

How many times could it do that?

I don't want to find out. Elise threw herself forward, leaned over the com-panel, and hammered the firing button.

Blue sparks shot from the speeder's wing guns.

In seconds, two flares lit up the skull's right cheek—then cooled. No apparent damage. "Oh, great."

The skull's nostrils flared. An ear-splitting explosion deafened Elise, and this time, she slammed shoulder-first into the starboard wall. Fire spit and fizzled on the floor, and Georgia screamed.

Elise wheeled—and saw Georgia hanging half-in, half-out of a wide open tear in the speeder's starboard wall. *Pa* slithered over her cousin, trying to cover the breach, but it wrapped around Georgia instead.

"No!" Elise grabbed Georgia's arms and pulled her inside. Elise's hands stung, then burned like crazy as the *pa* slid over her flesh. Georgia screamed again, this time in agony, and Elise joined her.

Sweet mercy. The *pa* was burning her up!

And it was burning Georgia, too.

Elise had no idea what to do.

Georgia's skin went from red to white to red, and her cries matched Elise's. They struggled to scrape off the *pa*, but it clung like hot glue.

Bright flashes of silver and black lit up the cabin. The speeder shook and groaned, but Elise could no longer understand what was happening. Her brain blazed with pain as her skin twisted and split.

Ki! Where are you? Help us! Oh, God. Help us!

* * * * *

Ki roared in frustration, terrifying the priests assembled on the Tuscan Platform.

"*Shanna*!"

"Hold him," Akad instructed, jerking the chain attached to Ki's neck collar. His eyes darted to the assembly of witnesses growing in the clearing, and even Ki's befuddled brain knew that the high priest was weighing the feasibility of letting Ki escape.

Arda had reacted with shock and horror to the announcement that their Sailmaster had been abandoned. And yet, each village had dispatched a witness, as per the Law. All were gathered, save for three, from the farthest regions.

Once the witnesses had all convened, the execution was to proceed—never mind the Fleet and the Home Guard, already engaged in the heavens above.

The battle for Arda had begun.

No one wanted to lose Ki now, and yet, their beliefs, the Law—if they stood firm in custom and tradition, would Arda not be rewarded, as had always been the case?

Ki growled and pulled against his collar. Not in cowardice. Not because he feared to die. Because he could feel his precious Elise, close to him. In distress. He could hear the screams of his unborn daughter.

"She is dying." He pulled Akad toward him. "Let me go. I must save her. Let me help Elise, and I will come back here and hand you my head!"

The lesser priests murmured. Akad fumbled for the keys to the chains, but the witnesses broke out in angry murmurs.

"I—I cannot release you," Akad murmured. "Though my heart would have it so."

A shout rang out. One of the remaining witnesses had arrived.

In frustration, Ki closed his eyes and reached out to Fari's thoughts.

The Fleet was taking heavy fire, and giving it, too. Plasma blazes lit dark space, outshining stars. OrTan skulls flamed and careened. Galactic gunboats whirled around Fleet frigates. Ki had Fari's vantage point on the helm of *Astoria.*

The line was holding. At least for now.

Astoria swept alongside a skull.

Fari bellowed and drew his barbed blade.

Ki's own diamond blade burned at his side. Would that his hands were free! He would slay his way to Elise, and then to the Fleet. To his brother's side.

Krysta. Ki turned his attention to his sister. *Where are you? Have you found her*?

No answer came to Ki. Not even a whisper.

Disturbed, Ki struggled to connect with the *pa* on Krysta's borrowed speeder—or on her rightful one, piloted by Elise.

Still, nothing.

What had happened?

They weren't—they couldn't be—

"No!" Ki's cry of anguish filled the Tuscan clearing.

Along with it rose two more shouts. The final witnesses to the execution, arriving at long last.

*****

Elise came to awareness, lying on her back, on the deck of the speeder.

But wait. It wasn't her speeder. The top of the ship was intact. No *pa* curtain winked against the stars.

And there were swords and blaster guns scattered all over the silvery metal floor. They clattered as the speeder lurched and shot forward, presumably toward Arda.

Elise checked for her daughter, who felt safe and warm in her belly. All was well, at least in that respect. Then, she sat straight up, squinting in the darkness. "Georgia?"

"She is unconscious, but not injured," said a cold, hard female voice. "In the back hold. I eased the pain of her burns, as I did for you."

"Krysta!" Elise got to her feet, but her legs buckled. Every muscle in her body ached, and her cheeks felt like someone had seared them with a brand.

Krysta stood over the companel, keeping her back to Elise. Forcing her throbbing limbs forward, Elise moved toward her, but held back at the same time. Her sister-in-law was angrier than she imagined, and she didn't know what to say.

"The skull ship—" she began, but Krysta cut her off with a wave. Like Ki might do, if he were that mad.

"Destroyed. I carried two plasma grenades, on the off chance you would make it back. We have no wing guns in exchange, however. If we don't make it to the Fleet side of the line before we're detected, Gith's forces will render us to dust."

"Why did they attack?" Elise reached Krysta's side, but Krysta didn't look at her.

"Over you, of course." Krysta's tone sliced into Elise's heart. "Treachery, bribery—they have the Council behind them. But none of that matters. We have to get to Camford, to the Tuscan clearing, the Platform. There might be time to save Ki."

Everything around Elise seemed to stop, even though they were moving faster than she could comprehend. "What are you talking about?"

"We have a law on Arda, Elise. The Law of Keeping." Krysta kept her eyes straight ahead. Her voice remained as icy as a Nashville January. "If the Sailmaster's woman abandons him before Presentation, he is not fit to rule, and must be put to death to make way for his heir."

"You've got to be kidding." Elise's ears started to buzz. "That can't—you wouldn't—Ki's people wouldn't—no."

"They would and they will. They may have already."

Elise scrubbed her palms against her hot cheeks, her tearing eyes. "Ki never told me that! Any of it. I wouldn't have left him if I'd known, not for anything."

"You should not have left him, irrespective." Krysta pounded a fist against the com-panel. "It was wrong of you, and if he dies, I do not know if I can forgive your cruelty."

The pain in Elise's limbs turned to incredible heaviness. Dread. Grief beyond measure. "Go faster," she whispered. "Fly us to pieces if you have to."

Krysta hesitated, then punched a few keys. The speeder trembled as it picked up velocity.

Elise gasped as Arda sprang into view.

They dropped like a stone into the atmosphere and shot across the moonlit sea. Over the beach, over thick treetops. Warning bells sounded—and then a horrible crash rocked the entire craft.

Elise cried out as Krysta pitched forward. A yawning hole opened in the speeder's viewing window, sucking Krysta out, over the com-panel. Elise tried to hold her, but burning metal and dripping *pa* hammered her hands. Krysta slipped slowly from her grasp—thigh, to knee, to ankle.

A giant skull shipped loomed out of the darkness, rounding to open fire again.

Just as suddenly, a magnificent silver frigate dropped out of the sky, streaking to intercept.

Screaming like a banshee, Elise rooted for the frigate to blast the skull to bits. She braced her legs against the com-panel base, refusing to surrender her grip on her sister-in-law.

And then the speeder's engine's sputtered—and died.

The ship hung for a long second, then plummeted toward the trees.

"Christ!" Elise's heart thundered in her throat.

Damn the fire. Damn the *pa*. Damn the OrTans and foul luck and stupid ancient laws. If they crashed and died, they would by God do it together.

Elise rocked back on her heels, pulling at Krysta with all of her remaining strength. "Get…in…this…ship!"

* * * * *

Ki Tul'Mar hadn't struggled as the *Ord'pa* forced his neck to the chopping block and chained him to the loop on its surface—but he struggled now to see the fireworks in the Eastern sky.

The battle had come planetside, and this gave even the die-hard law followers pause. Some were thinking to let the Sailmaster live a few moments longer, if only to turn back this threat.

Akad was certainly of this mind. Of course, Akad had been doing everything within his priestly powers to draw out the execution.

Ki was grateful, until the moment he could no longer sense his wife, his child, or his sister. Thinking so many of his heart's family dead, he wanted to die himself—but then the stars caught fire.

And Ki thought he caught a glimmer of Elise's life force.

Forcing his way to his feet, pulling at the chopping block's ring with his bull's neck, Ki snarled at the red-robed *Ord'pa.* The poor lesser priest stepped back, even though he was armed with a double-bladed axe and every muscle in Ki's body wore a chain.

Reaching his thoughts to all available *pa,* Ki located a crashing speeder. With lives inside. He couldn't read them well—Elise, but not Elise. Krysta, but not Krysta. And another. Primitive, yet not primitive.

Not bothering to sort it out, Ki flung almost the full force of his psi power into slowing the ship's descent. He left only enough energy to keep the Fleet sailing. The rest went to his task.

In his mind's eye, the blazing bubble of *pa* skimmed treetops, coming closer—and then his actual eyes could see it. A twisted, mangled piece of a speeder.

The crowd gasped and murmured.

Ki guided the flaming bubble to a halt above the Tuscan clearing, and lowered it to the ground beside the Platform.

Immediately, the priests and witnesses set about putting out the flames, using coats and psi power and what water could be had.

Akad leaped off the platform and waded into the ruined ship—but quickly ran back out again, screaming like a hog at slaughter.

This caused the *Ord'pa* to raise his horrid axe beside Ki.

At that moment, the crowd around the speeder fell away. Many yells and shouts could be heard, and then Ki saw the reason.

A woman came stalking from a rent in the dead ship's side, wielding a great emerald sword above her head.

But not just any woman.

Ki's mouth fell open in wonder.

Lorelei. *By the Gods. The* Lorelei *have come*!

Her clothes were torn and smoking, leaving her barely clothed. Great tendrils of *pa* marked her hands, arms, chest, and face, ending in stark flame patterns about her smudged, desperate eyes.

And yet, this wild woman looked and felt familiar. The curve of her hips. The grace of her walk. The wild abandon of her moon-kissed blond tresses.

Elise. It had to be Elise.

And yet…not. She was changed. Different.

As she approached, Ki realized that somehow, Elise had merged with *pa*, like a true Ardani. Raw *pa* had touched her, and yet instead of burning her or killing her as it would most primitives—or at best touching her and fleeing when put down—the universe's life force had joined with her flesh and spirit.

How could this be?

More screaming filled the clearing, this more untamed than the bestial noises coming from Elise.

Another naked female left the smoldering wreck. This one was firehaired and pale, but also covered in magnificent *pa* designs. She held not one sword, but two ruby blades.

A third woman, oddest yet, followed. This one was completely silver, soaked in *pa*, iridescent in night's cool light. And she bothered with no simple blade or dagger. No. This one held two blasters, one in either hand.

Krysta?

Ki had no time to ponder the meaning of the strange sights before him, as Elise had reached the Platform.

She climbed the steps slowly, and lesser priests scattered in every direction.

The *Ord'pa* trembled. His axe rattled in his hand.

Witnesses crowded back, away from the avenging spirit.

Ki stared at his beloved, and tentatively reached for her thoughts.

Shanna?

Elise's silver-framed eyes blazed as she looked at him. Her mind joined his, and the force of her rage nearly blew

Ki off of his feet. Her sword still glinted above her head, and she locked her hands on its hilt.

"You—you bastard!" she roared, and brought the sword down with the force of a thousand warriors. The blade smote the chain binding Ki to the chopping block. Sparks flew, and the chain's links exploded.

The rest of Ki's chains fell to molten dust at his feet.

Below the Platform, the firehaired *Lorelei* let out a whoop and rattled her dual ruby blades. "Y'all want some of this? Come on!" She stamped the ground. "Who's your mama? Huh? Who's your mama now?"

Krysta—or the being who was once Krysta—shrieked as she leaped onto the Platform. Her blasters leveled on the *Ord'pa.*

The red-robed priest threw down his axe, vaulted off the Platform in a billow of cloth, and fled into the trees.

At this, Elise whirled on the crowd, magnificent in her *pa*-enhanced beauty. Ki felt his mast harden to the point of pain, despite the circumstance.

"I am Elise!" she shouted. The resonance and menace in her voice forced the crowd back another few steps. "*Shanna Ki Tul'Mar*. Consider me Presented, damn it, or else!"

Chapter 12

Elise soaked in Camford's deep, fragrant bath. The clean Ardani water soothed her singed skin, and the healing oils Akad had given her faded her bruises, sealed her cuts, and eased the ache in her muscles. Vapors rose around her, filling her nose, lulling her increasingly active baby to sleep in her belly. Her hair stretched beside her like a wet pillow as she drifted, and she studied herself in the tiled ceiling above.

Her body was whole and healthy. Nothing broken or too terribly damaged. And yet she was changed, fully and completely. Silver flames decorated her hips, reaching inward toward the light triangle of curls between her legs. The same pattern outlined her breasts, flicking toward her nipples. It climbed her neck and spread across her cheeks in thin lines, blazing out around her eyes.

Strange. And yet, not ugly. Exotic, in some ways. But different.

She could feel it, the *pa* mark. It felt warm, exciting, and alive. It stimulated her if she turned her thoughts toward it, even for a moment.

Akad had examined Krysta, Georgia, and Elise after the Presentation ceremony had been officially completed.

Georgia was fine, though marked with *pa* like Elise, all over her perfect, delectable body. The pattern her silver designs took reminded Elise of honeysuckle or climbing roses, and she loved how it twined around and through Georgia's full nipples and red hair—above and below. At the moment, Georgia was resting in the infirmary, under

Akad's care, slated to begin lessons in Ardani culture tomorrow morning.

Hope Akad does as well with the…um…sexual freedom issue as he did with me.

Elise took a deep breath and let the water close over her face for a moment. She liked the silence. The soothing rock of the water as she moved.

It reminded her of a woman's embrace. Georgia's, or Krysta's.

God. Maybe one day, both of them at the same time, with Ki watching. I might have to tie his hands.

That thought forced Elise's hand between her legs. She pressed against her aching mons, and her body convulsed almost immediately.

What a fantasy. Though it might take some time to come true.

Krysta remained under the high priest's ministrations as well, recovering from overexposure to *pa*. She had been caught in the speeder's hull energy as they crashed. Because of Ki's connection to the *pa*, it would not let her fall, nor release her once they landed safely, because her wounds were too great to leave unbound. The *pa* literally held Krysta together and refused to let her die.

The price for such extreme measures was high, and Krysta would need a rest of many stellar days before she felt like herself again. The extra *pa* would stay a part of her, for at least a time, and maybe always.

When Elise had kissed her sister-in-law before coming to the bath, she had marveled at Krysta's iridescent skin and hair. It was like looking into a rainbow, deep and beautiful and wonderful. Akad said it might fade, but Elise almost hoped it didn't. Not if the *pa* felt as good to

Krysta as it did to Elise. Being covered in it like that must feel like being wrapped and soothed by the softest of blankets. Or like living in an OrTan pleasure bed—the one thing those stupid alligators could do right, after all.

Elise smiled a wicked smile as she thought about the OrTans and their arrogance. Fari and the Ardani Fleet had made mincemeat of their finest skulls, and they had limped home with only two functional ships. Lord Gith was still alive in all his mangy glory, but the Galactic Council had reversed its decision to support his claim. Partly because the Galactic Council had three ships left to their name, too. But mostly because new information about Elise and Georgia had come to light.

It seems the reason Elise and Georgia had little family on Earth was because at least one of their parents hadn't come from Earth. Akad had suspected it when he saw the *pa* marks—something he assured them simply wasn't possible for primitive humans. Genetic testing had confirmed his theories, and also demonstrated a splash of Earth DNA in the Tul'Mar bloodline. Apparently, there had been some cultural mingling. Warriors sampling forbidden fruit—or the forbidden fruit wishing on one too many stars.

Elise and Georgia were half primitive, half Ardani. *Lorelei*, as the legends held. And they were related, though only distantly. Cousins, many times removed, as they had been raised to believe. Krysta wasn't a true halfling, but she had enough primitive in her to interest every single warrior on Arda.

Because of their Ardani blood, Elise and Georgia were members of a race exempt from claiming by any man, save one of their own choosing. And so Lord Gith lost any right to complain, and he took his broken skulls and went home.

Within hours, word spread all over Arda of the coming of the *Lorelei*, and how Elise had fought for and laid claim to Ki Tul'Mar. All stains on Ki's honor vanished, and once more, his people worshiped his mind's breath in their sails. Elise had completed the ceremony, still filthy from her flight, by making her swirling handprints on the Wall of Life and speaking her pledge to remain by Ki's side, always.

And then she had come to the bath alone, daring Ki to follow.

She was still mad at him.

Why didn't he tell her about the Law of Keeping? He had almost been beheaded. She had been so terrified he would die that she almost jumped out of a speeder in the middle of the Ardani atmosphere.

And afterwards, all he did was stare at her, gaping at her *pa* marks and mumbling, "*Lorelei,*" over and over.

Men.

Honestly.

And warriors.

Ardani warriors were like…men times ten, or something. Even Fari had been a clod after *Astoria* docked. Staring at her. And staring at Georgia like she was a fresh piece of meat. Akad had to have Fari carted off by a bunch of sailors, just so Georgia could get some peace and rest.

Elise sighed and brushed her hands over her skin. *Pa* tickled her palms.

She supposed she was clean enough, but when she left the bath, she knew Ki would be waiting in the bed chamber. No doubt he had bathed somewhere else, in five minutes flat. No doubt he was stretched out on the pillows, displaying his sculpted muscles, his cock hard and throbbing, waiting for Elise to submit to his charms.

This image made her *pa* channels pulse, and her hands traced them to her nipples. They ached. The rest of her ached, too. For Ki. She wanted exactly what he did, and she knew it.

After one last dive and swim around the bath, Elise got out and toweled off. The soft Ardani fabric was sweet torture on her sensitive places, and she barely took the time to push her damp hair behind her ears before she left the bath chamber.

Ki Tul'Mar was indeed waiting right where Elise thought he would be, in exactly the state she imagined him.

With no shame, she stared at his high cheekbones, his ebony hair and eyes, his hard chest—and his hard cock.

What a magnificent man.

From his heavy-lidded gaze, Elise knew Ki thought she was magnificent, too.

"Come here," he demanded. "I have been too long without you."

Elise responded to his edgy, husky tone with shivers. She walked slowly toward him, running her hands over her nipples and pinching. Dropping her fingers to her wet, curly hairs and touching her pussy where she knew he could see.

The moment she reached him, he grabbed her hands, pulled her down, and gently rolled her beneath his strong bulk. Her wrists were trapped as he lowered his lips to hers, but not unpleasantly trapped. Like a playful challenge. A sweet claiming.

And then his mouth did claim her, totally.

She opened her thoughts to him, and their minds joined with a jolt. A full Ardani joining, like Elise had so deeply wanted.

And God, was it worth everything, and then some.

The full measure of Ki's love flowed into Elise. His dreams, his sensations, his pleasures—everything he thought and felt were hers to share at that moment, and she willingly gave him access to every corner of her mind and soul.

"Never leave me again," he whispered. A plea, not an order.

Elise let him see how she never planned to be away from him. Not for a stellar hour. Not for an Earth minute.

"No more secrets," she murmured.

Ki responded with helping her delve farther into his thoughts, so deeply that she knew his every secret and hint of a secret—and found that there were no nasty surprises, waiting to hurt or frighten her.

His lips traveled from her mouth to her neck, tracing and nibbling the flames of *pa* coursing over her. Elise moaned at the feel of his teeth on her flesh, biting what ached and screamed for his attention. Her *pa* marks warmed to blazing, touching her intimately with Ki, increasing the flow of pleasure and energy between them.

Still, he held her wrists above her head, and Elise writhed in his grip. The pleasure was almost too much, but as they shared it, it became bearable. Ki's mouth found her nipple and fastened on, sucking deeply. His tongue raked against the hard, tight flesh, and Elise cried out, halfway to orgasm already.

Ki let go her wrists at last, to grasp her other nipple in his strong fingers. He pinched as she had done to tease him, but firmly. Elise arched beneath him, begging him with her body. Pleading for him to keep going, down to where she needed him.

He did, but he took his sweet time, kissing every inch of her along the way. Pulling her skin into his mouth. Caressing her curves. Licking hollows and dimples. When his fingers finally sank into her pussy, she came immediately, thrusting against the gentle pressure of his palm against her clit.

Before the aftershocks finished, he buried three fingers in her wet slit and ran his tongue over her swollen bud. Elise jerked and groaned, lost in the skill of his mouth and hands. In minutes, he brought her to two more orgasms, all the while sharing his love-struck thoughts and sensations through their psi link.

And sharing his fantasies, too.

In response, Elise sat up before he could enter her, smiling as she took his thick, hot cock in her hands. Stroking it like he wanted, up and back, gently, then faster and harder, eyes open, staring straight into his.

He came with a deep groan, and she slid down and took his already-hardening cock in her mouth. His salty taste filled her senses, and she loved it, just as she loved him.

The feel of his swelling cock in her mouth thrilled Elise. Ki sat on his haunches above her, rocking as she sucked, taking him deeper and deeper into her throat until he came again, shaking as she drank down what he had to offer.

Ki's breath came in jagged gasps as he pulled himself from her lips, lifted her up on the pillows, and bent to kiss her. The combined smell of their sex made her heart beat faster, and she opened her legs.

With a sigh of complete satisfaction, Ki rubbed his soft cock against her welcoming slit. In no time, he hardened again, and she arched back, lifting her hips to accept him as he plunged inside.

"Yes. Ah, God." Elise wrapped her legs around him and held him for a moment, savoring how he filled her pussy, basking in his feelings of perfection and joy. Then she opened herself wide and turned loose her thoughts. Letting him know how fast, how strong, and how completely she wanted him.

Ki growled with delight and rammed into her.

She couldn't get enough, even when she lifted herself to slam against him.

More, she pleaded. *Fuck me harder!*

In a frenzy, Ki pumped as hard as he could, pulling Elise's hips to meet him. Over and over. Harder and deeper.

For a long moment, they were one mind and one body, pouring their essence into one another, until they both saw shooting stars and exploded with screams and groans and boneless gasps.

Elise welcomed Ki's spent weight on top of her, and held him close.

Never again would she let this man go. He was right where he belonged.

* * * * *

Ki woke to find his *shanna,* his *Lorelei,* still beneath him. His cock was hard again, begging for relief in her sweet quim. And yet Elise's sleeping face was so peaceful, so beautifully exhausted, he was loathe to disturb her.

Sensing his thoughts and desires through their complete psi link, she stirred, just enough to open her legs and draw him inside her slit. As she woke, he was rocking her gently against him, and she smiled.

"Yes. Don't stop. Yes." Her hips lifted from the bed, then her legs splayed wide. Ki put his hands on her wrists because she liked that, and quickened his pace.

Elise rewarded him by groaning and bucking, demanding more. And he gave her more, hammering against her soft quim until she moaned with pleasure and release. In seconds, Ki found his own release, spilling himself inside her until he had nothing left.

Or thought he had nothing left.

Elise wasted no time kissing him, running her nails along his back and his buttocks, cupping his tender sack in her skillful fingers. When his cock quickened again, she rolled to her knees and offered him a choice of pleasures. This time, he took the tighter entrance, gasping as her ass closed firmly around his throbbing length.

He pulled her to him, slapping flesh on flesh, gently at first, but she urged him on.

"Don't hold back. I can take what you've got."

Elise's words lit a fire in Ki, and he worked her masterfully, plunging in, pulling back, and using his hands to knead first her nipples, then her swollen clit until she screamed. And scream she did, only moments before he climaxed with a loud bellow.

And still the Sailmaster's woman was not satisfied.

She bid him lay down, which he did. With short, unabashed sighs of desire, she straddled his face and worked her quim over his tongue and lips. Honey and musk. Her scent filled him as he found her wet slit with his hand.

Elise eased her quim up and down on his fingers until she came again, and again. And then she turned and used her mouth on his cock, drawing the last bit of his seed from his loins in one hot, long spurt.

Ki fell into a sleep like the dead, knowing that when he woke, they might eat or bathe—but they would surely start again, enjoying the depths of each other's soul. His heart felt light, and glad, and grateful.

This is as it should be. As it always should be. And I am the most fortunate man in the universe.

Epilogue

Two stellar weeks after her timely arrival back home, Elise rested her hands on her swelling belly, gazing across the spacious, rolling lawn of Camford. Ki's strong chest made an excellent recliner, and Arda's soft grass felt like silk against her bare legs. She was wearing one of Ki's tunics, and that was all—as was customary for a happy pregnant woman.

Servants bustled in the distance, cleaning walks, polishing statues, and pruning plants. Since the Ardani Fleet overwhelmed the combined OrTan and Galactic forces, and since the *Lorelei* had made their presence known, there had been renewed patriotic fervor and planetary pride. Ki had to turn away people wishing to serve the Sailmaster and his growing family.

Overhead, the crystal sky gleamed, and big sun shone beside little sister with no clouds to block them. Elise enjoyed the light whisper of unborn Katryn's thoughts. She couldn't make them out just yet. A hodgepodge of sensation, really, but definitely the mental stirrings of a secure and healthy infant-to-be.

"I think our daughter is eager to be born," Ki whispered in Elise's ear. His rich, deep rumble gave Elise pleasant shivers as his hands cupped and gently squeezed her breasts.

"Don't tease." She nudged him with the back of her head. "You know Akad already restricted us from sex. Slightly different biology, too many energies, crash trauma—all of that bull."

"He is a worrier, that priest." Ki sighed and relinquished his hold. "I do not know how I will survive prolonged celibacy."

Georgia came into view in the distance by the main gates, holding hands with Krysta. They spied Elise and Ki, waved, and changed direction to join them. Krysta's skin had returned to its normal rich shade of brown, but her hair retained the changeable silver from her *pa* exposure. She was still a walking rainbow, and Georgia's honeysuckle and rose *pa* markings glittered in the suns as well.

Ki groaned. "More unbearable teasing, to have the three of you in one spot, and no chance for relief."

"Behave." Elise grinned. She knew Georgia and Krysta had been getting friendlier, and she hoped it had gone much further than playful touches and kisses—but she didn't know yet.

Georgia wasn't saying much, except *keep that man away from me.*

Meaning Fari, of course.

The Sailkeeper of Arda had found his soul's mate.

Only his soul's mate was none too sure of the massive, self-assured, spear-toting second in command of the Ardani Fleet. Because they were all planetside and not in desperate straits, the relationship could follow a more traditional course. A true Ardani courtship, with all the trappings.

Elise was loving it. The songs, the bouquets of wildflowers left outside Georgia's door. The long looks over expansive dinners.

He's arrogant and obnoxious, Georgia kept saying. But she also kept looking, at his muscles. At his dream-dark curls and night-black eyes. Elise had no doubt that Fari would win her cousin over and have his prize.

Sooner, rather than later.

Krysta was having less trouble with Georgia, as the two found common ground in the care and training of the lovely Chimeras. Elise enjoyed watching them ride together. The way they held each other, and moved like one body on the Chimera's slender backs. She liked watching them kiss, too. Just like she knew she would enjoy seeing Fari and Georgia kiss.

One day, soon. And after I give birth, look out. Ki and I—and our family—will be very, very busy people.

Georgia and Krysta approached them laughing, and settled on the grass beside them. Georgia bent over and kissed Elise on the lips, lingering for a moment, as they had been doing since Georgia learned the freedoms and privileges of her new life. Krysta went next, lingering longer, until Ki groaned and pleaded for mercy.

"You are all unkind, to torture a warrior so," he grumbled. "Where is Fari, anyway? I assumed that where fair Georgia tread, my brother would be close behind."

"He is turning out the herd," Krysta said. "Best to keep him busy."

Georgia sighed. "I so don't want to talk about this. I know y'all think we're a match made in Heaven—or wherever Ardani good folk go when they die—but I'm not so sure."

He's very well endowed, Elise thought, directing the sentiment at Georgia, along with a mental image of Fari's well-honed physique.

"Hush your mouth. Um, brain." Georgia punched Elise lightly on the arm. But she was smiling. Elise could tell she was interested. Scared, but fascinated.

Krysta lay back on the lawn. "The Festival of Seasons approaches soon. You will have ample opportunity to know Fari better then, sister-to-be."

Elise raised an eyebrow. "I don't know much about this festival. Tell me more."

Ki coughed, then laughed.

Krysta laughed, too. "Trust me. You will like it."

Georgia went a little pale beneath her silver markings. "Will I?"

"Oh, yes." Krysta rolled to her side, winked at Ki, then took Georgia's hand. "I suspect it will be the best week of your young life."

At that, Georgia blushed and covered her face. Krysta gave her a playful hug and kiss, and the two snuggled into Elise's side. She stroked their hair, and leaned back against Ki, enjoying the weight of his arms around her.

He was definitely the most un-boring man in the known universes. Slayer of Elise's First Rule, and Elise's Second Rule, too. Ki would never make her yawn, and she trusted him totally. Elise's Third Rule stayed intact, though. She would always take care of Georgia—but not because Georgia was her only treasured family. Simply because Elise loved her so dearly.

If life got better than this for the Sailmaster's woman, Elise didn't know if she could handle it.

But she sure would try to find a way.

The Arda Collection

Glossary

Akad	High Priest of Arda, marked with *pa* like henna tattoos on his cheeks.
Arda	40,000 stellar years old. Home planet of Ki, Fari, Krysta, and the Royal Fleet. It is famous for its metallurgy, fine castles, magnificent Chimera, and towering warriors. Arthurian in rule and structure, but enlightened and modern, Arda has an excellent reputation in the Free Galaxy. Ardani citizens carry pa-marks, and most are psychic. The generous and respected Tul'Mar clan has ruled them for thousands of years.
Astoria	Flagship in Arda's Royal Fleet.
Bandu	Fierce purple fighting women, valued by OrTan slavers.
Camford	Palatial ancestral home of the Tul'Mar clan.
Camford Forest	Thick woods surrounding Camford's grounds.
Chimera	Multicolored horse-like creatures native to Arda, with giraffe and unicorn features.

Coscans	Blue aliens often enslaved by the OrTans; females have a single breast.
Denovan	Furry, manlike, very stinky aliens. Often make use of OrTan pleasure slaves.
Elise Ashton	28 Earth years old, blond hair, blue eyes. Dreams of a spacepirate rescuing her from her boring life.
Fari Tul'Mar	Sailkeeper of Arda. Brother to Ki and Krysta, guardian of the Sailmaster and the Royal Fleet. 120 stellar years old, marked with *pa* in the shape of a great winged bird on his chest. He carries a barbed, spiked sapphire blade.
Fergilla beasts	Ugly, hairy white buffalo-like beasts native to Arda, often used in name-calling and insults.
Festival of Seasons	Ardani celebration of the harvest. Involves mating of unwed citizens.
Galactic Council	Ruling body of the known and free planets. Mediates disputes, but has some vulnerability to treachery and bribery.
Gasha	OrTan pleasure bed.
Georgia Steel	28 Earth years old, auburn hair, green eyes. Distant cousin of Elise Ashton's, raised as her sister.
Ki Tul'Mar	Sailmaster of Arda. Brother to Fari and Krysta. 150 stellar years old, marked with *pa* in a flame pattern

	beginning at his waist, dividing on his chest, and flaming up both shoulders. He carries a diamond blade that matches his *shanna*'s eyes.
Kon'pa	Ardani Dance of Life, to honor *pa*, the stars, and the sails of the Royal Fleet.
Krysta Tul'Mar	Captain of the Ardani Home Guard. Sister to Ki and Fari. 100 stellar years old, marked with *pa* in a soft pattern like cherry blossoms on her chest and neck.
Law of Keeping	Ardani law governing the claiming of a Sailmaster's mate.
Lord Gith	OrTan prince and slaver.
Lorelei	Three mythical guardians of the Tul'Mar line, halflings, often depicted as feral with cat-like features.
Nostans	Tiny species, approximately three feet in height, who frequent OrTan pleasure ships.
Ord'pa	Ceremonial Ardani executioner.
OrTa	Planet in the Free Galaxy still engaged in the forbidden and heavily policed practice of pleasure slaving. OrTans are large and humanoid, but scaled.
OrTan collar	Collar used on pleasure slaves to ensure compliance through pain. Also translates multiple languages for the wearer.

OrTan pain stick	Long staff with electrical tip used for subduing OrTan pleasure slaves.
Pa	The living substance that created and makes up the life force of the universe.
Royal Fleet	Ardani space frigates, sloops, and speeders commanded by Ki Tul'Mar.
Sha	Ardani soul's mate (male).
Shanna	Ardani soul's mate (female).
Skull	OrTan combat or pleasure ship (slaving vessel), shaped like a humanoid skull.
Tuscan Platform	Ancient site of Ardani rituals, located in the center of the Camford Forest.

About the author:

Annie Windsor is 37 years old and lives in Tennessee with her two children and nine pets (as of today's count).

Annie's a southern girl, though like most magnolias, she has steel around that soft heart. Does she have a drawl? Of course, though she'll deny it, y'all. She dreams of being a full-time writer, and looks forward to the day she can spend more time on her mountain farm. She loves animals, sunshine, and good fantasy novels.

On a perfect day, she writes, reads, spends time with her family, chats with friends, and discovers nothing torn, eaten, or trampled by her beloved puppies or crafty kitties.

ANNIE WINDSOR welcomes mail from readers. You can write to her c/o Ellora's Cave Publishing at P.O. Box 787, Hudson, Ohio 44236-0787.

Also by ANNIE WINDSOR:

- Arda: The Sailkeeper's Bride
- Legacy of Prator 1: Cursed
- Legacy of Prator 2: Redemption
- Redevence: The Edge
- Equinox anthology with Katherine Kingston & Vonna Harper
- Cajun Nights anthology with Samantha Winston & Patrice Michelle

Why an electronic book?

We live in the Information Age—an exciting time in the history of human civilization in which technology rules supreme and continues to progress in leaps and bounds every minute of every hour of every day. For a multitude of reasons, more and more avid literary fans are opting to purchase e-books instead of paperbacks. The question to those not yet initiated to the world of electronic reading is simply: *why?*

1. *Price.* An electronic title at Ellora's Cave Publishing runs anywhere from 40-75% less than the cover price of the exact same title in paperback format. Why? Cold mathematics. It is less expensive to publish an e-book than it is to publish a paperback, so the savings are passed along to the consumer.
2. *Space.* Running out of room to house your paperback books? That is one worry you will never have with electronic novels. For a low one-time cost, you can purchase a handheld computer designed specifically for e-reading purposes. Many e-readers are larger than the average handheld, giving you plenty of screen room. Better yet, hundreds of titles can be stored within your new library—a single microchip. (Please note that Ellora's Cave does not endorse any specific brands. You can check our website at www.ellorascave.com for customer recommendations we make available to new consumers.)

3. *Mobility*. Because your new library now consists of only a microchip, your entire cache of books can be taken with you wherever you go.
4. *Personal preferences are accounted for*. Are the words you are currently reading too small? Too large? Too...ANNOYING? Paperback books cannot be modified according to personal preferences, but e-books can.
5. *Innovation*. The way you read a book is not the only advancement the Information Age has gifted the literary community with. There is also the factor of what you can read. Ellora's Cave Publishing will be introducing a new line of interactive titles that are available in e-book format only.
6. *Instant gratification*. Is it the middle of the night and all the bookstores are closed? Are you tired of waiting days—sometimes weeks—for online and offline bookstores to ship the novels you bought? Ellora's Cave Publishing sells instantaneous downloads 24 hours a day, 7 days a week, 365 days a year. Our e-book delivery system is 100% automated, meaning your order is filled as soon as you pay for it.

Those are a few of the top reasons why electronic novels are displacing paperbacks for many an avid reader. As always, Ellora's Cave Publishing welcomes your questions and comments. We invite you to email us at service@ellorascave.com or write to us directly at: P.O. Box 787, Hudson, Ohio 44236-0787.

Printed in the United States
22117LVS00007B/259-351

9 781843 607373